BIRD -
SELF

ACCUMULATED

BIRD-

SELF

ACCUMULATED

Don

Judson

NEW YORK UNIVERSITY PRESS
New York and London

NEW YORK UNIVERSITY PRESS
New York and London

Library of Congress Cataloging-in-Publication Data
Judson, Don, 1950–
Bird-self accumulated / Don Judson.
p.   cm.
ISBN 0-8147-4229-7 (alk. paper)
I. title.
PS3560.U375B57   1996   95-50173
813′.54—dc20   CIP

New York University Press books are printed on acid-free paper,
and their binding materials are chosen for strength and durability.

With love to my mother and to LeAnn

CONTENTS

ACKNOWLEDGMENTS

I would like to thank Barbara Epler for her wonderful job of editing, and Phil O'Connor and Howard McCord for believing in me, though I often gave them reason not to.

Parts of this book have been published in *Descant* and *Happy*.

THANKSGIVING,
1979

I had decided to borrow someone's car for a drive down by the water. The place where I worked at the time—it was a hospital for emotionally damaged children—couldn't have been more than a couple of miles from the bay. My whole job consisted in being at my room by nine o'clock and waiting there to evacuate C and D wards as well as 9-North in case of fire.

But I went to find the security guard and bribe him with two of my pills.

"What are they?" he asked.

"Can't you see the blue and green specks?" I insisted.

We were on the second floor hallway and I didn't want Nurse to come walking up unexpectedly.

"Listen," I urged, "it won't take long. An hour at the most. I might stop, get out at the picnic benches—what could happen?"

He held the pills cupped in his hand underneath a lamp and moved them up close to its bulb where they looked like teeth polished and set side by side.

"Are these those things that were going around last summer?"

"Right," I agreed although in actuality I could not remember where the pills came from, or when.

"Because those were all cut with rat poison."

"You're kidding?"

"Uh-uh."

"Well, these are probably from a different batch. They're good."

And it was true. My head already felt as if it had been broken up into some kind of powdered substance. I could see right through the darkness into where autistic children lay asleep dreaming, though I could not imagine what those dreams might be or if they were even anything you or I would recognize as dreams at all.

Somehow I got lost. I drove up and down staring at streets whose names I remembered but now looked like different places altogether. I kept finding the same abandoned filling station. It was a cinder block square, busted out and with concrete pads where grew a series of wires capped and shut—but out front of its parking lot someone's belongings were stacked sidewalk to sidewalk in a neat semicircle with a chair at each end, and several extension lines had been run through the alley

BIRD-SELF ACCUMULATED

from some other building's window for a lamp; beneath it, a man in green sweats and a baseball cap worn backwards and lined with tinfoil fingered the band of a ruined watch while mumbling sternly at the lines of passing traffic as if we were, each one, rude and ill considered guests.

And at this street's other end, where it narrowed, there was a bar; and here, people who could not understand their own fate stared out toward the rest of us from behind slightly darkened windows. Soon, most of them would be back in jail. It was that kind of place. Some of the same ones, my comrades and road dogs, stood around at the corner waiting for something, anything. I recognized them all. And several did call out. But when I pulled over, these people only seemed to turn on me with murderous intent for a moment and then disappear, or were not really there at all to begin with. It reminded me of a time when I was no more than six and my mother and father had a party. We lived in the suburbs then; my father and another man were in business together—they ran a funeral home— and the plan was for us to move into a huge apartment right above it, but that never happened, and soon in fact my father was kicked out of the business and was gone anyway on drunks more than he was with us and we could barely afford to live . . . but on this night there

DON JUDSON

was a party. I'd been shown around a little, the kind of thing adults love when they're drinking—the cute boy in pajamas serving peanuts and such—and after that I was put to bed. But at some point I woke back up. I was frightened. The house had gone silent, and for several minutes I lay not moving, but finally got up from bed and began down the hall to the basement where the party had been held.

At the mouth of the cellar stairwell I hesitated, unsure—what if my parents were gone, If no one were in the house and I was there alone? I bent to peer down the stairs searching out partway along the cellar's backwall a lampbase, and in its thin shadow of light, set on several books, an old, black, extension phone.

I was terrified it might begin to ring.

All of this went on just as if it were in my sleep because I can recall now a faint mist beginning to cover everything inside the house. It was soft against the floor and wallboards. Against feet, hair, eyes. I could taste it along my tongue. Everything stood out.

Listen, it said.

Listen.

I went to the doorway and then out into the yard. The hedges, trees, driveways and homes of my neighborhood were there just as they'd been before but I couldn't find a name for a single one of them.

BIRD-SELF ACCUMULATED

All of it had been set off balance.

The borders erased.

There was no way of understanding even where my body ended and the rest picked up. Can you imagine such a thing? How a person can step outside their own life? That's how I began to feel driving the security guard's car around and around on that street. I began to feel as if I might be taking place inside a television movie.

Finally, in desperation, I found a new turn and went along until it brought me out beneath a highway underpass which I recognized as being on the complete wrong side of the bay from where the park was. Factories appeared everywhere. They lit up into the sky like a carnival. I felt about them as a person who had been strangled and thrown away to be forgotten. But something happened then. In the distance I could see the black line of water. Clouds seemed to come down all at once over it. They were across the bay. Then snow began.

Our first snowfall of the season!

It fell in large, steady flakes which thickened against the windshield and road, and filled me, stupidly, with a vague sexual desire—I believe I've woken from wet dreams in just such a way, apprehensive, as if some undeniable truth about myself had been carefully and irretrievably made known; yet now I'd not even been asleep, and, humiliated, needing as much to move as sensing in the snow an opportunity, I dimmed the car's lights and made my way unnoticed between two lines of razor-topped fencing and a guardshack, and snuck this way in surrounding darkness down an access lane. . . . Heading, I knew, toward water, past walls of what appeared to be coal, and wide scars of land gouged flat where pipes sprouted and intersected at random—far off behind or to one side, smokestacks, ghostly, looming wraithdrab; and then to a place where these as well ended and there seemed to be nothing but vast skeletal night, and through it or up into and stamped upon, a constant falling, falling, and so without chance to see or react, unable to stop in time, found myself run out of road and driving headlong, axledeep out onto the tide-flats of the back end of the bay.

The car coughed and died.

There was no other sound at all.

Off to the right I could see a series of concrete breakwalls where rats the size of poodles romped like hungry children. Beyond them was a ruined liftbridge. Snow fell softly against it, and fell and softly settled on the water, and mudflats and road, erasing, and traffic in the distance—

I seemed to be very far away.

BIRD-SELF ACCUMULATED

Out in the harbor itself, about two hundred yards offshore, lay on its side the immense hull of an oilboat sunk just that summer past.

It raised up as if it were God. And I think now that maybe it was. I pushed open the door and made my way toward it through the thin lights of the security guard's car and along the stand of mud and broken stone strewn with bottles and slender fishline, and down then to the oily black and cold water which was completely still, and heavy, and not so much reached up as shifted to accept my falling into: first ankle . . . then thigh, and waist; until I bent forward to it fully.

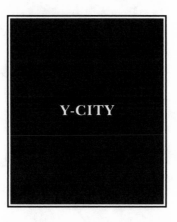

Y-CITY

Cheech suggested we burgle a house.

"We can stab the walls again," he said. "Shit in the refrigerator."

I had no idea what he was talking about. But our Marlboros had run out and the sun was beginning to make my teeth ache and all around us objects continued moving in ways they weren't supposed to. The street especially, it was up in my face, and then down. Which isn't the worst. The worst is like what happened in June when I'd been tripping for several days and then decided to do a hit of speed and hitchhike to the lake. Beaner said: Whoa man, you don't look so good. Yet the way all of it had been going, for the first time I'd felt entirely scraped clean. Everything in town had sat boxed up close looking bright and plastic as if it had just been washed. A shutter kept clicking across my eyes. I saw Beaner right in front of me at about sixty frames per minute. She was small and beautiful and all strung out. For one profound moment secrets popped between us in our blood and brain cells and then I woke up on a hospital room emergency cot. My hands had been tied to the railings. Some allergy pills from a back pocket were arrayed across my chest.

"How long have I been here," I asked.

"You've had a seizure," someone told me. "You're doing fine . . . you talked all the way over here in the ambulance."

"You've been sitting up," they said.

The room had been filled with people I couldn't even remember.

"I thought I was still hitching to the beach," I informed them.

Today was different. Not necessarily better. I'd drunk some cough medicine to get the codeine. On Sunday. At first it was okay, we were at the bowling alleys, but then I kept getting higher. I sat down outside by myself for a while to see if it would stop. But it has ended with me unable to attend work for three days.

I mean, how can I?

At night I dream faces at my window. I sit up with my insides in my mouth from fear and see nothing and finally say, "Whew, it was just a dream." Then, as soon as I relax, a face comes right back into the room saying my name and I'm up yelling, stuck inside a dream I've

BIRD-SELF ACCUMULATED

already dreamt is over. It has become a problem to the point that whenever I lay down I begin to hallucinate. At least when I'm up and around I feel like a piece of shit but it is a feeling I can relate to.

Only, now, Cheech wanted to ask me such a question—

"Burgle," I said to him. "Do I look like a person who would care to burgle a house?"

We'd come by this time to find ourselves in the front parking lot of the dry cleaning place. Cars kept driving in and out. There was a noise like the ocean ascendant inside my head and Cheech sat beside me during all of it as if he had an ability never to be fooled. "Check it out," he explained, "this place—we don't even have to break, we only just got to enter."

The house belonged to a doctor. We drove a long way from the road to even see it back there in the trees. Cheech finally shut the car off next to a stone wall. Although he was smiling he'd done a lousy job. There were leaves in the windshield wipers and a willow branch from his having nodded off and run us into some bushes just as we'd left the main road.

Right before that the radio had been playing my favorite song.

"Hurry," I'd warned him already knowing it was too late, "wake up."

"I think I took the wrong turn," he said.

Where had he gotten such an idea? I wanted to point out that we'd already driven right across a stream. By the time it was over, besides a broken windshield and fenders left behind, the car had gotten part way up a fallen tree.

"You push," Cheech suggested. "I'll steer."

I had sat staring in amazement at the fact we were still alive.

"One, two; one, two," he'd called out.

Yet as soon as we were safely parked, Cheech seemed determined to forget this incident altogether. He pulled up next to the stone wall and climbed happily out of the car and pointed to the house.

"This is it," he said.

"Home sweet home," he proclaimed with an expansive flourish.

None of it felt that way. You only had to look across the unbruised lawn and neat checkerboard flagstone patio to the house itself, all great rising shingled sides of weathered wood and fine cut glass, to know that if anyone were to come along they would understand Cheech and myself right away to have been puked up in the exact wrong place. I didn't know what to say. A smell of

BIRD-SELF ACCUMULATED

flowers came up mixed into the heat of gasoline. It was all I could do to keep from gagging. Things didn't seem all that much better out in the country.

"Oh shit," I wanted to cry.

But Cheech was already standing inside the doctor's foyer punching numbers to deactivate his alarm system.

I was astonished. He'd walked right in.

"Karin," Cheech told me, meaning his girlfriend. "Guy used to be her stepfather."

Behind him, further back into the hallway, the ex-stepfather's paintings and jewelry and television sets were neatly stacked.

"We've been here about three times," Cheech explained, "since the family went on vacation."

The entire house was a mess. I wanted to check the bathroom cabinets but Cheech insisted on a tour to point out all the places he and Karin had been doing it. These places included beds and couches and end tables. They had done it in most every room and even the sink. The thought of that, of Karin sweeping silverware and plates from the counter as Cheech hoisted her over its edge, left me dizzy. I remembered her from coming into the Hilltop one afternoon for a drink: she looked to be a person who could have you moaning two weeks into an icehouse.

People had actually stopped playing pool.

DON JUDSON

"My, my, my," some of the boys said when they saw how she was inside a pair of pants with a zipper running down the length of her hip. It was a zipper they'd wanted to believe themselves right then and there to have fumbled and cried over night after night.

Now I thought I sat down from the idea of her in a sink only it must have been the codeine because when I looked around I wasn't sitting at all but standing instead in the cellar where there was a game area. Cheech was gesturing all around. Then he turned and left. After a minute music came from the living room. There was no hurry is what it seemed he'd said. We could load the ex-stepfather doctor's belongings into the car later. There was no hurry at all.

Only something had changed. A sudden shift in the geography of my high. I could no longer stand still. I walked to the second floor expecting lights and cymbals and the sound of God. Instead there was a room filled with rifles. They were beautiful. One of them looked to be the kind used by snipers. I took it down and found some bullets and went to a window.

All of this took place as if I were inside a dream.

The ocean still buzzed.

My legs were weak.

There was a fan which someone had broken and a

BIRD-SELF ACCUMULATED

night table by the window with a long silver mirror on it. I sat cradling the rifle in my arms. Through its scope, one mile away, toward the lake, everything appeared to be neatly and exactly framed like a toy. I watched for a while as salesmen, housewives, and visitors to our region drove their station wagons or sports cars down and around tiny, wooded hills. It was as if we had all climbed inside a diamond together. I could smell those people! Every hair plastered against their wet foreheads. The sweat as it dripped or ran down faces, dark, then pale— across shadows thrown into small, quick bursts of light.

My finger was right there on the trigger. It might have been exactly what I'd been waiting for, but I'm not sure. I remember taking a deep breath.

Nothing moved.

All the clouds sat above the grey sludge of our famous lake. The sun was a piss yellow ball. It sat there too.

Then, finally, downstairs the music went off. I heard Cheech snoring. Snoring! Who could guess, I've heard people say on many occasions, what the fuck that dude is even thinking. Once, just after he'd returned from Vietnam missing a kneecap and some other parts of his leg, Cheech tried to set an Italian on fire. It was at a gas station. The Italian's girlfriend had that hot look about her with big hair and jewelry and so the Italian, who thought Cheech worked at the station, said, Hey gimp—how about it.

That was a wrong thing.

He did not understand Cheech's kneecap lost in a tunnel where it had been blown up while he crawled and crawled after the enemy. Can you imagine that, moving and moving into something about which you have no idea? Cheech could, and so he put the nozzle of the gas pump right inside the window of the Cadillac where the Italian and his girlfriend with big hair sat.

This all took place during a time when it seemed that every week on television you saw another Saigon monk burn themselves in protest. So when Cheech soaked him down the Italian still tried to look hard, "Hey," he said, but he must have been thinking right then about those Buddhists. How they bent the air. And died folded inward like kerosene flowers. Because as soon as Cheech showed a book of matches the Italian was over his girlfriend and out the other window.

What is there to know in this life anyway?

That day we robbed the doctor turned out to be a good one. I went and woke Cheech and we put the jewelry and televisions out on the flagstone patio and

BIRD-SELF ACCUMULATED

then loaded them into his car. By then my high was
finally running down and when we got back to town an
edge seemed to be off everything and we'd made some
money so there were drinks and a few laughs together.
There always were with Cheech. I thought of him as a
person who knew me better than most.

But in 1975 he was to hold a pistol to my head and
make me show him where John the Chink and I had
hidden our crystal meth. The gun looked so amazing
there in his hand it made me cry.

"Shut up," Cheech said.

At first he only slapped the barrel across my face
but then a fit of some kind seemed to take hold and the
gun went off four times.

"Don't worry," he insisted after the ringing had
stopped and I'd told him what he wanted to hear, "nobody's been shot."

The idea seemed to disappoint him.

Although I haven't seen Cheech since, I heard from
Karin that he might be down south. They'd been mar-
ried and when things began to go wrong and after he'd
robbed me and some other friends and disappeared, she
got an unsigned postcard from Key West, Florida. Karin
talked to me about all of this one night on Dexter Street.
She was drunk and played with her wedding ring a lot.

DON JUDSON

After a while she asked me to go home with her and I did, though it wasn't about revenge, and besides, by then I'd become a person who could barely stand the thought of someone else touching them, and none of it really mattered anyway.

IN SECURITY
LOCKDOWN:
PRISON,
1981

When Boo-Boo stabs Morris Boyle I am reading a news magazine that someone has smuggled onto the wing. It is an article about a dog who uncovers a grave of several small bones wrapped carefully in bits of waxed paper. The dog is not a police dog but only one which happens to be digging by a gazebo in a neighbor's garden. Also recovered are: three black candles, tufts of hair, a ring and two decks of playing cards. The woman who owns the gazebo and the gardens has lived alone for as long as anyone can remember.

She tells a story which begins: Before you knew me, a stranger, a religious man of cosmopolitan background. . . . It is a ridiculous story, and no one listens to her. This is in a part of our country cut off and burned dry by a drought of several years so you'd imagine its trees to hang like sticks from the sky above the old woman, and the sky itself absurd and the dog as they stand there surrounded by reporters, she already having been recorded as feeling herself to be the victim of a cruel, if ultimately harmless, high school prank. It is this close community of small towns, and teenage drug abuse, she mentions more than once. But that evening, in a sprawling pond behind her home, police detectives called to the scene discover a child's head sunk in a bag of stones.

Around me, the weather has turned drizzly and hot. Sometimes with a small polished mirror held outside my bars, I watch the hall. I'm waiting. And I wait and nothing changes. There is only silence or an unbroken noise. The silence is a prayer. Of surrender. To this, I whisper, to this and other devotions.

I don't know.

What is there to tell here in security lockdown I eat breakfast. Lunch. Dinner. Do some push-ups. Like a holy man of days I jack my dick testifying to the bars the walls and ceiling. Then wait for mail call, medical rounds—for the nurse or med-tech who will pretend not to hear at all if I speak; and for the fat guard delivering letters cell by cell, calling out our names. . . . He is more direct, but crazy as well, warning me every day that no one can expect to return from prayer alive.

My mother again writes that she is frightened. She puts more locks on her door.

I wish that I could help.

But there is no message from here, there is nothing.

BIRD-SELF ACCUMULATED

Although maybe I should tell her this: embrace, like the many heads of one snake, your fear. And: walk out to meet it.

I'm not sure, I don't believe I should say anything at all: but listen, around me the weather has turned. It has turned the walls to sweat like crack like wine like sick. They sweat roaches, and they sweat my life unreal. Please, calls Boo-Boo every afternoon, Mother of God allow me to die.

Go ahead.

Listen.

Hey dude, you don't have to ask permission. Just do it, alright? Do yourself and shut the fuck up.

But of course he doesn't. Instead takes a piece of straightrazor to Morris Boyle. Oh God, is what the Boyle yells.

Oh Jesus shit, he says.

There is a road around the prison and in the summer dust will cover it by noon and on the day I was taken to lockdown I watched the Sergeant and a co-1 come down this road, which was already hot and dusty and settled itself behind them as they walked. I had been doing sit-ups. Three sets, then rest for five minutes. From where I sat I could watch along the fence line for a quarter mile to a point at which the ground climbed and the road turned and went out of sight, the trees across from it stunted, the sky low and hot and punching down into the road. Then the Sergeant and Mr. Mays came down past the trees and onto the compound. Tampa Fats, acting as a spook for a poker game, warned the players. But the cops walked past Fats and the game and up to me.

The room where I was taken was small and tight and without air. There were three of us in the room: myself, the Colonel, and an investigating Lieutenant.

"Now, we'd look a little foolish, wouldn't we," the Colonel said, "knowing what we do, and letting you back on the compound?"

Behind the Colonel's desk was a Coca-Cola machine. Its lights had been busted out, and over the door someone had hung a picture of a woman with holes where her face was supposed to be. Above it, on the wall, a deer head and two photographs were hung. The first, of men in army uniforms. Four guards whose faces were blurred indistinct posed together in the second. Between them they held a bowling trophy. A banner across the bottom of this picture read: Department of Corrections. Four Rivers, C.I., 1986. Near the Coca-Cola machine there was also a coatrack and a fan. That was all there was in the room. The fan did not appear to be working. It was very hot.

"The facts are, son—" the Colonel said, "and here's number two, the first being we have every reason to believe the contract on your life . . . you see? But the second being that the man who has come forward—and here I'm just thinking of you, son—the man dealt with no more than a go-between, and this is where the problem lies and where you can get out of the problem . . . it being to tell us who the perpetrator or perpetrators of the contract are. This is what you can straighten out right now."

Everyone was being very pleasant. When I'd first been brought into the office the Lieutenant had looked up at me from where he sat on a corner of the Colonel's desk and asked if I would like the handcuffs off. "Well now," the Colonel told me, "seems we got us a little problem and some confusion both." The Colonel appeared to be about sixty years old and was thin and tall and formal in a southern manner which made him seem very pleased to be having this conversation. But he was not at all happy. "A five hundred dollar contract," the Colonel said. It was as if we were all friends. And now they would have me locked down twenty-four hours a day under administrative confinement until I could be shipped because I was white and because I had people and possibly a good lawyer and if they let me back onto the compound I was going to be killed and that could cause them trouble. So of course everything was decided and there was no reason for anyone to be unhappy, except me, who did not count, and the Colonel perhaps, who did, and who had already been inconvenienced by this bit of paper work and because of that wanted names and would not be pleased if he did not get them.

"A five-hundred-dollar contract," the Lieutenant repeated.

Through a window which had recently been cut into the wall of the office and left unfinished I could see the road the Sergeant had walked down a short while before, and beyond that a field of cut stumps. Ten or twelve prisoners were in the field. Several of them worked, pulling stumps from the ground, while the rest stood waiting beneath a stand of cottonwoods which had peeled and were rotting in the sun. The men who waited held picks and shovels in their hands and looked down and did not appear to speak to one another. Only once had I found trouble while in this prison. The first day in a nontransit dorm, I was sitting on my bunk, just unpacked, but with three shirts and my sunglasses still lying on top of an upturned box when a big jitterbug called Cocoa and three of his running partners came up

BIRD-SELF ACCUMULATED

to me. "Hey man," Cocoa said, "them ours," pointing
to my sunglasses. I'd seen Cocoa around before. One
morning, turning a corner behind the education building, I'd come upon a group of inmates watching a robbery. It was Cocoa, who had an old man down on the
ground and was kicking him, working his legs, laying all
his frame into every kick. Everybody just stood around
and watched. "Easy now, cracker," Cocoa told me that
day in the dorm, "real easy." One of the homeboys
Cocoa had brought with him wore a gold tooth and
touched a spot on his lip just above it and then adjusted
the brim of his cap so that it sat sideways on his head.
Underneath the hat was a red bandanna.

"Them me, cracker," Cocoa said again and then
slowly reached down and took the sunglasses.

"Alright," the homeboy said, laughing softly.

That night after supper I had sat on some bleachers
by the baseball field until I saw Cocoa go into the dorm
alone. I waited a minute and then walked to a blind spot
between the dorms and the fence and dug around a
large rock, pulling it from the ground. Underneath was
an eighteen inch long piece of re-bar I'd stolen from the
machine shop and buried a few days before. Holding
the pipe through a hole cut into my pants pocket I went
to the dorm and found Cocoa sitting on one of the
toilets in the large shower room at the back of the build-

ing where, at that time of day and if I was quick, there
was little chance of anyone coming in on us. The toilets
were separated from each other only by small brick
partitions, chest high, and left open at the front, and I
walked up on him before he knew I was there and
began without a word to swing the re-bar. The first time
Cocoa was hit he screamed and his eyes rolled back into
his head. After that he only made small wet sounds
and was probably mostly unconscious, although once it
seemed he was trying to get an arm up to protect his
face. There was blood everywhere. "Whose sunglasses
are these?" I kept asking Cocoa.

Later, I cut the name tags from my clothes and
pitched them and the pipe into a laundry cot. I had
never been more frightened in my life. But this, now,
would have nothing to do with Cocoa and it would be
much worse. I knew that immediately. On the streets I'd
robbed cocaine dealers. Now they'd found me and had
contacts in this camp and there was nothing to be done.
It occurred to me for some reason then that what I was
looking at—the road, now empty, and the clean line of
fence, both somehow unreal against the sky, and behind them the sky, immediate, as if someone had
painted it on a white sheet of paper and laid it inside my
mind—these would be the idea of prison I'd always
carry with me.

BIRD-SELF ACCUMULATED

"I don't know, sir," I said. "You depending on me
. . . it would seem to make you the one got a problem."

How many times has one voice come toward concep-
tion—moaning under the weight of light, and the voice
itself no more than a moment's absence of that light?

Once, when I was nine years old, there was a fire at
a horse stable. It was March and patches of snow were
still on the ground. Several horses had escaped the
barns by kicking down their stall and then stable doors,
and when these—some three or four only—rose suddenly from the frozen woods they themselves had become the fire, their manes and steaming flanks, and
most especially the rising cold of all their eyes.

Blood sweated and splayed out onto the snow. I was
only nine years old and wanted this to stop and began
praying, but from the barns all that could be heard were
whistle-pitch screams of terror—and I remember seeing
myself then as both the horses which remained trapped,
and the uncontrollable wall waiting before them.

Now, here, swallowed within this prison if I could
only make for myself a geography of fire distinct somehow from fire—

"Don't bitch up," we call to one another.

"Don't break weak."

DON JUDSON

Boo-Boo stabs Morris Boyle and I believe there is no difference, but the day burns thin as parchment to display an engine of living spread between ribs—and me, who sits alone and shakes to death here in my cell.

He stabs Morris Boyle and I can taste and see through to the sweat of weakness, waiting—but not for me. . . . Because daily I kill myself, scouring clean intestines, kidney, liver—and lay them singly across my bed, one after the other. And all I wonder is this: how is it that one of us becomes bone-white with want, and the other not?

This is what I mean: prison, to me, has become the first clean mirror. And can only be what it is. In the mirror this is the heart of midnight. With a sheet propped under my head as a pillow, all night I stare at the bars. I stare the bars, which are green, into nothingness. Then stare them into the world's last hard bands of light. Then I step beyond the light: I'm standing in a clearing at a wood's edge. Behind me is the prison. The moon sits bunched above it like some great catbird. It's a high summer moon, yellow and finely veined. A cloud passes across its face. And for one moment I'm no longer a man standing outside a prison but am again a young boy rowing his skiff. It is a July night smelling of salt marsh, and from our front porch my parent's voices drift, threadlike and disembodied, across the water as if

BIRD-SELF ACCUMULATED

they were issuing from the darkness itself which leaves imperceptible not only the porch where I know my mother and father sit but our house as well and even the shore, only a line of lanterns strung from posts running the pier's length to anchor my imagination as I move along the vast black lip of an open sea, yet all the while believing not in any terrors, but instead in the finality of those lights and that shore, and of the voices behind them. On that night also, lying against the gunwale, shivering slightly, my shirt damp with oil and water, I watched high flathead clouds cross in silence before the moon, and was in that moment as sure of the equable passage of the world as I've ever been. So now, standing just beyond the barbed wire fence I try to find again, waiting in this memory, belief, and hold it to myself a long minute. Then I draw a deep breath of air sweet with orange blossoms and walk away from the prison compound.

All night I walk, twice skirting marshy areas. Close to dawn I think I hear the dogs and crawl into a thicket which opens slightly around the trunk of a tree. All day I wait and sleep in there. Once, when I wake, my eyes will barely open. They are swollen and oozing. My skin feels warm. Asleep again, I dream of insects large as bats. What stops this dream? Is it the dogs, can I hear them? Later, I sit up and become sick. My legs are swollen from bites and the poison of nettles. But it's dark again. I start out. By midnight I've gone at least ten miles. Now my hands begin to turn blue. It seems I can picture myself drinking some time earlier from a dirty pool. I try to reconstruct events in my mind, yet can't. Just before sunrise I stumble from a steep bank onto a small dirt road wound like a ribbon down through the darkness. At the end of the road is a tiny cottage. I stand up once more, carefully, and begin to walk. While my legs seem to move, I get nowhere. Finally I sit down in the middle of the road and begin to cry. A door swings open at the front of the cottage. An old man comes out. He walks down the road and lifts me in his ruined arms.

Is this how light death is, I wonder.

He speaks gently and tells me that fever has burnt the very being, and its weight, from my bones. Mr. Ghede is his name.

In his room lingers a dry sweet taste. I'm sitting at a table, Mr. Ghede at its other end. Before Mr. Ghede waits a pencil and a piece of paper with which I've asked him to draw a map of the woods. He wears the cokethick glasses of the nearly blind and if my limbs weren't swollen to inhuman proportion I would hit Mr. Ghede and rob him. The old man places a steaming mug of broth in my hands. He will help me.

BIRD-SELF ACCUMULATED

Mr. Ghede puts his face up close to the pencil and paper, peering at them. Drink the rest, he tells me, it will make you feel better.

I notice there's a pond behind the cottage. And gardens. The old man has built a doll-house half again larger than his own quarters. After that, time must pass because the room becomes different. It is lit by candles placed in each of the four corners. I can see into the light. The roof and walls rush down to the floor.

Mr. Ghede stands outside a window. I see him watching. First there is this: the heavy smell of flowers. They are in my mouth and on my tongue like nettles. I gag and fill the air with petals thick as wings. The old man has put something in my drink to do this. As I look he turns into terrible Mr. Bones and then becomes an old woman without teeth.

He chuckles. Goat's blood, he says. Now he seems to be watching my face. Goat's blood, and wine and something special to give you vision.

I hallucinate a graveyard. The old man comes screaming about his life's sleeping mind, talking like one hundred mouths and calling his name to be Baron Cimetiere. I can't let go. Electricity has crucified my head to this picture. Of the staring angels and the stars which bow down. And Mr. Ghede. He's smiling. The old man is different than the other dead. He has sharp

DON JUDSON

little teeth with which to bite and the pain of cancer is on his inside. Then I know him to have done something terrible. And he begins to speak. Come in, he says. Come in, come in, he sings. Come in.

> Mr. Bones is waiting, he shouts, wanting to read
> each one, the story of their doom
> and cuff their little ears and ring
> their little ears.

Everything falls away from me.

When I open my eyes I've been tied to a chair. Mr. Ghede sits directly in front of me. A doll is on his lap. He explains it to be our soul which he's carried in his angel heart like a broken stump chamber of salvation. Then he touches its waiting eyes to mine, my hair and my mouth.

As Mr. Bones, he explains, he had no face at the shopping mall.

"They'll find the head sunk in a bag of stones."

And Mr. Ghede has indeed become beautiful. A blue light surrounds him. It trembles. I can see words fall out of his mouth as he speaks them.

"A young man's head in a bag of stones."

There are one hundred, maybe one twenty—it's difficult because of changes, how some cells they double up,

BIRD-SELF ACCUMULATED

some not, but there are about that many of us in security lockdown. Mostly on rule infractions or investigation, the rest, one reason or another, have asked for protective custody. So, maybe one twenty. It is a corridor of two wings, back to back, thirty-five yards long. Each cell two and a half paces across. Three lengthwise. In stacks at the head of my bunk I have matched three pair of underwear, two shirts, two pants—the shirts and pants, blue—three towels and one facecloth. This is how my day goes: at four o'clock someone throws shit on a med-tech and gets banged up in a strip cell. I listen. Then lie on my bunk, exhausted with hate.

My father would want blood and the pain of redemption.

He, however, is dead.

It may be important to realize that my father once gained some small share of fame in a country band singing on stage about drinking men matching their lives to the empty days of a city. No one believes this, he had a reputation as a minister-type of sorts. But there you go, every weekend he wore long string ties and white shirts with red and gold phoenixes over each pocket to a club in downtown Boston on a street close to its Combat Zone. During summer afternoons, hookers, young girls from Ohio and Tennessee would stop in for a drink or dance before going to work. They giggled and paired off like shy children.

"Look at the teardrops," my father sang to them, "running all down the streets."

He was eighteen years old.

I don't know.

Actually, he never sang.

He was a minister. That's how they met. It is another part of the country, one dry with dust, and my mother is in the audience. She is beautiful then.

Or, she is ugly. Or dead.

And he is an undertaker.

They never meet at all . . . save once.

As for myself, I am living in prison.

Sometimes, listening to the days sweat themselves dry against the grey square plexiglass skylight fifteen feet away out in the corridor I imagine myself, while pulled into this cell, waiting out too the same rainstorm in a bar with vodka tonic and country girls and outlaw music on its stage.

Otherwise, after two free letters for the week and a pack of Bugler rolled into cigarettes I'm out of options. During the morning it's quiet. Then someone will start. Yo, whiteboy. Or nigger. Anything at all.

On the afternoon Morris Boyle had first been brought to security lockdown everyone got up on him

BIRD-SELF ACCUMULATED

fast, as they did whenever a new man came down. This was about two o'clock. Hey baby, it started. Come to daddy. And then they were all up on the bars—What is it mamma oh whitebread whitebread, whistling slung hip and eyes, testing, and it turned out him being slight and frail, meaning nothing, but also in protective custody and having asked for it himself his first day down. Which is what he told real quick. How two niggers stole his Reeboks. Then came back later about some jewelry—

Why didn't you . . . , Danny Spencer began.

Boyle asks him: What? Get stabbed over some watch, there was something I was supposed to do—it was all completely out of control.

The whole wing began rocking. He seemed to be exactly what they were waiting for.

That night I heard Gregory Angels, who was in the cell next to him, running the facts down to Boyle. "Man, you already let yourself get run off the compound. . . . Everyone gets tested. . . . And they know, my friend; what they know is you can't live in p.c. forever. Sooner or later you got to go back to population, and when you do, they want you thinking you're more afraid than you really are. That you got to hook up with one of them . . . that you got to, so might as well do it now. Someone to look over you, you know what I'm saying?

DON JUDSON

"You will be giving them cigarettes, you will be giving them money. You will have a daddy, and anything he wants, belongs to him."

It did no good.

They gave Boyle a name. Holly, because he was from California and to them that meant Hollywood.

"Come on, Holly," June-Bug told him, "why you checked in? Come on out to my cell, you be safe."

And then Country Cool soothed, "Fuck them niggers. You my friend, I get out there—no one on the compound gone mess wit you."

Always trying to run that smooth shit.

"What you think you'd do if I was in your cell," Boyle asked, and they loved it. They all laughed, saying they couldn't tell him, they had to show him. And every time he was taken to shower or sick call, every time, the whole cell block got on the bars talking that shit. But Country Cool was different. He was in love. Flat out in love. Had Boyle cut out and owned, and talked real soft, sweating in the heat, and he'd moan, "Oh Holly, what they gone do—what they done wit you now, baby?" All day long he ran his game, mostly soft, sometimes with that real easy threat you hear in prison, and always making Boyle believe that he knew him better than he himself did. "Oh Holly, what they done wit you, baby?"

BIRD-SELF ACCUMULATED

Boyle couldn't take it. A week after coming down he was ready to sign himself back onto the compound. The cops made him fill out a form saying he no longer felt his life would be in danger, and then upgraded his status to administrative confinement and moved him out of his segregation cell overnight while the paper work was processed. They put him in with Boo-Boo. We all knew what was coming, and waited.

And of course it came.

I don't know. My beliefs may run counter to what you assume. I enjoyed none of this. It wasn't all that long before Boyle was brought back to protective custody from the hospital. This time they moved him into the cell next door. Two cops walked him down. Mine is the last cell on the wing. Everyone had an even closer interest in him now, and I didn't like to see it. He might have been alright if he'd fought when Boo-Boo tried to take him off, that alone could have done it. Sometimes, fighting once will give a man the heart he needs. But he hadn't. Boo-Boo tried to force him—he had a shaft of straight razor bedded in a pen and its point was sharpened, but it was mostly for slashing. Boo-Boo had stuck Boyle once or twice, and then, when Boyle fell into a ball screaming for the cops, he'd really gone to work, cutting him across the face and arms. That was how the guards found them. Boyle bleeding pretty good and rolled into a ball. . . . Boo-Boo, who is not right in the head, more confused than anything else.

At mail-call on the same day they brought Morris Boyle back to lockdown the fat guard asks what I would've done, he has two letters for me in his hand—"Listen, he says, "if you'd found out about the contract before we did . . . what then? Maybe think about asking for protective custody, huh?"

He holds the letters just beyond my reach. "And what about after leaving here," he asks. "If it follows right along—anywhere you're transferred . . ."

Nickerson is his name. He holds my letters chest high. He wants me to look at him.

This is what he'd like me to think about: how it would be about money, period . . . if I was in population there would be no one person to go after—nothing I could do to make everyone stand back. And every night, sleeping in an open bay dorm—less than two feet between row after row of double bunks, the bunks themselves and clothes hanging and string lines making the whole dorm a blind spot. . . .

"We can't see shit, my friend," he tells me.

"Who would it be," he asks. "Sooner or later . . ." Nickerson shrugs his shoulders.

BIRD-SELF ACCUMULATED

I believe Nickerson when he says there is little enough hope in prayer. I also believe—fuck him.

Maybe because of what Nickerson says Boyle decides that he and I are the same. Boyle is wrong. It is this way with Boyle: he could have fought.

Boyle is just showing himself weak.

One night, about ten-twelve days after that, Boyle must have heard me pacing. The rest of J-Block was silent. It was three o'clock into the morning. "Ain't this something," he asked, and the voice startled me. Between the shared wall of the two cells and the grille gate, in a space of several inches, I saw Boyle watching me. His hands were held out from his sides, palms up, and he looked all around himself. "Ain't it," Boyle repeated as if he should be conceded a certain disbelief at finding himself in protective custody. This is what he wanted. Justification. And to form an alliance.

"Ain't this really something," he asked.

I wouldn't help. I won't be one of those circling like a dog smelling blood. But I wouldn't help.

"I don't know," I told Boyle. "I don't know about all that shit."

Yet I'm happy enough to have Boyle to talk with. On the compound I'd had books, mostly on history, and so each night after it gets quiet I begin to talk and for the most part he is willing to listen and picks up on ideas. Sometimes he ruins it by not following and then saying something stupid. But other nights he seems to drink it in and even points out this or that inconsistency. Which I don't mind. Enjoy in fact. Only then he forgets. Trying to be clever, he wants to make it something else. "Homeboy lays it out like numbers . . ." he says, "but it's you. I can smell it. I can hear *you* going cold right through these walls."

That makes me angry and I get real quiet. Because he should understand. Already. It is **this this this**—not homeboy, not knowing, not any shit which might expect something later. Who the fuck is Boyle anyway, he should be glad I speak to him at all.

So I get real quiet. To remind Boyle, but this time it doesn't faze him at all.

"Check this out," he tells me, "I was up the Panhandle. A small town out along the beach . . . the ocean and everything. At night all the time feel as if you could expect something. I'd been . . . see, there were a lot of well-off women. Divorced. Widowed women; forties and so, and they hit the clubs. Sooner or later I thought I'd hook up with one, hit something big. I like the clubs too. So, I'm out. I'm at a table and this woman comes over. Just like that. Don't even look at anyone else. Sits down and wants to know if I got some coke. And I know this woman. I know . . . you understand? *Her*. 'You a

BIRD-SELF ACCUMULATED

cop,' I ask. Which of course she isn't. The woman is just nervous. I think this is not her thing. Any of it—the dope, the bar scene? But she's made up her mind . . . about this, decided. So, I ask if she's a cop and then bust up. Relaxing everything a bit . . . I *am* going to get the dope, right? Only, she wants both of us to go—come right along with me. Okay, even better. Of course we end up at her house, a condo. I've never seen anything like it. The woman owns—check this out, she lives on the entire top floor. There is a jungle outside her living room. A regular jungle, okay? The trees and all. Forty stories up. Her entire living room, windows. When I got out of the car it was just morning. 'Up there,' she said, pointing, and I got out of the car and right in front of me was the whole package. I told myself, I said, 'this is it brother. . . .'

"Anyway, when we get upstairs I had the shakes a little. Been up most all the week. But I fix us a real good shot of coke to cure all that. Wham. Now I was feeling good again, thinking my luck is changing—the woman, she ain't bad, looks like she might be pretty good in bed—I'm digging on the apartment, out on the balcony, you know? Thinking this is all of it and I turn around and the lady is dead. She's on the couch, dead. At first I think, 'what the fuck.' This is not right. What am I supposed to do? So, I fix another shot. But I can't

get high with the lady lying there, so I pick her up into
the bedroom. Pull down the covers, put her in, go back
to the dope. It's morning. Out the window is sunshine
and the palm trees and all them people—and I know
whatever it is I gotta do I can't do it out there. Not right
then. What I end up, I find a VCR and I watch it. I
must've watched twenty-four hours straight. Steady fixing shots. After a while, the coke? You might as well,
you really can't move at all so I just keep watching.
Things do get crazy. Finally, I begin to believe I am
dying—I mean, I was scared, I thought to myself, 'oh
Lord, what is this?' My nerves like yanked goddamn
light cords. Outside, all the noise firing through tele-
phone poles and wires until the ocean and the beach
and everything out there turned to glass. 'Man oh man,'
I thought, 'so this is it. This is what it's all about.' And
laughed. But *I* wasn't having any of it. So I go to the
windows with tape and towels and face cloths. Put them,
stuff them all along the windowsills trying to catch everything and make it stop. I go into the bedroom, and
I've forgotten about the lady. . . . 'Holy shit,' I say. 'Jesus
Christ.' So, things are bad enough. But then they get
worse because above the bed, on the wall, in her mirror,
I see me. I am looking into my own eyes at real bad
dreams. My bones pushing me into someone else. And
here comes the future. Me looking at me. Let it roll

BIRD-SELF ACCUMULATED

is what *I* say. Let it roll. . . . That's the only history a person needs."

The night it happens his voice is the first I hear although somebody must already have been shouting for him to shut it down. But he won't stop. He is slap bugging up. By the time I come out of my bunk, rolls of toilet paper are being lit and thrown into the corridors. "Motherfucker," someone is swearing. The whole wing has come awake. Boyle is screaming over and again. He has balled up his clothes and sheets and set them on fire. Down the hall someone hollers "rock the wing," and right down through the steel frame bunks the shaking begins. They beat the walls, the bars, the floor. In the two-man cells I know they crouch in dark corners, watching, while they pretend not to, each other, yelling as if together—"Die motherfucker," screamed at Boyle, yet their eyes on the other man in the cell with them. I see Boyle's shadow immense on the wall. Then the guards come and pull him from the bars. I can hear them beating him. It goes on for a few minutes and then it stops and they leave. I lie on my bunk until the wing again becomes settled. The lights are turned down then and I can hear the guards outside their office and soon a door closes and there is nothing. After a while I

DON JUDSON

go and look into Boyle's cell. He's sitting against the far wall, one arm thrown up on the grille gate, his head resting on the arm. "Weak bitch," I say, "they going to break you down." And for one moment when Boyle looks up I'm unsure whether I'm accusing myself or him. The air remains bitter with smoke. Every now and then someone down the line coughs. There are small murmurings. Before me I see myself crouched like a waiting animal with the stink of fear on it. "Let it roll," Boyle smiles up. "Let it roll."

We stare at one another.

And then I turn, and walk away.

Late; that's what I think. At first I don't know what's awakened me. Then I separate a sound, a small brushing of air followed by three or four taps as if a signal. Very soft. Going to the bars, I'm looking into his cell at him—directly into his face, each time it is swinging abruptly toward me—perhaps looking at him for thirty seconds before I understand what I'm seeing. His shirt has been shredded and braided into a rope one end of which is tied to the top cross-section of the bars, and the other knotted at his neck. As his body twists, his feet brush against the grille. And I'm looking into Mr. Bones's face.

BIRD-SELF ACCUMULATED

Backed into a corner, crouching by the toilet, I whisper, "What they done, what they done with you now?"

"A skull in a bag of stones," he replies.

And in that moment I have a vision of these walls like a shock of strict flames—and I see, I know what I would tell my mom. I would tell her, "Leave the door unlocked . . . leave the chain undone at night and each tightly drawn shade open because I'm coming home." That's what I'd say.

PROPOSITION

I was standing around in front of a job I'd just been fired from when two friends of mine came along. They were in a brand new car.

"Jump in," they said.

We drove through the park watching girls from the college sun themselves on little blankets for a while, and then went down an entrance ramp by the river where we ran out of gas.

"Shit," the driver swore.

He got out and punched one of the windows.

"This kind of crap always happens," he explained. It appeared as if both of them might begin to cry, and to join in the sadness I brought up how I was newly unemployed just that morning. But I could not work myself toward any kind of true grief, and besides, neither of them seemed to know I'd ever had a job to begin with. In fact, I couldn't be sure they remembered who I was in the least.

Myself, one time I'd been left at a party from which

a person disappeared. The people who'd brought me had gotten in several fights and decided to leave, but I stayed on going from house to house—it was a neighborhood party in an area where forty-foot boats were docked in slips off back lawns—and I went along looking for something to steal and locking myself into one bathroom after another shooting up and puking until I was back at the particular place from which one of the owners had turned up missing. Everyone was worried because this owner was in a wheelchair and they figured he'd wandered off drunk. Seeing a chance, I pretended, along with a woman with whom I'd been in love, on and off, for at least four months, to form a search party.

"He could drown," we claimed, pointing to the beach.

But she and I ended up in the lounge of a motel. As usual I was running my hand up and down the small of her back. We had been doing that whenever we got alone, touching and making small noises.

"Ooh," I told her.

Inside the lounge, someone called my name. It was a couple sitting right up at the bar.

"Hey, holy shit," they said.

I stood there grinning with no idea who they were. My date moved around impatiently waiting to be intro-

BIRD-SELF ACCUMULATED

duced. She had raven hair and skin like fine tea porcelain.

"Someone's disappeared," I told the strangers, but
they ignored this and clasped me to them, shaking their
heads in disbelief. The woman studied me with warm
and compassionate eyes and repeated my name twice
and smiled at her husband who was smiling at me.

"I have no idea who you people are," I told them.

It was a strategy I'd decided on the last time I'd
been in a conversation with a person I did not recall and
had spent an entire evening saying general and festive
things to her while inside me a panic grew that at any
moment I would be found out as an impostor. I had not
been able to stop talking. Finally, in desperation, I'd got
her into a corner with our tongues in each other's
mouths when I remembered who she was.

"Beth," I said. "Beth?"

It was ridiculous. She had once been the baby sister
of a former friend. She was pure. A child. I remembered ponytails, cuts on her little knees. Who could
guess that such a girl might grow into a person groping
in the corner of a sad bar with someone like me?

"You're too good for this," I had sobbed into her
neck. But it was too late.

So I'd told the new strangers right up front.

"I'm sorry," I said.

At first they were laughing.

"The Bent Spoke, in Escoheag," they told me.

"Tombo. We'd all drive around in his red van. You were with Betsy."

It was true, I remembered the Bent Spoke from when I'd worked down in that area, but I had no ideas concerning them or the people they'd mentioned.

"Two or three nights a week," the woman said, incredulous. "Jenny Shacked. Clifton. Stuart—all of us."

I had no reason to doubt her, only my memory could not walk me past the front door of the Bent Spoke and then back out again later into the clear dark summer air sprayed with light, perfect that far from the city, and then in the parking lot climb me into a red van where I'd apparently had an entire and detailed history with this person and that and that.

"I was drinking a lot in those days," I apologized.

Yet it did no good. The woman began to look at me and my date suspiciously; I could tell everything had gone over into the area of anger. "The last time you were over our house," she offered, "you ripped a radiator right out of the floor in the bathroom."

I was already backing away.

"Who is that you're with anyway," the husband called after us, "someone else's wife?"

BIRD-SELF ACCUMULATED

Which had been true enough. Her name was Judy and I'd imagined she would leave her husband and that I wanted her to, though in fact I only saw her once or twice again before she moved to Chicago with him and had something terrible happen to her which was written about in all the newspapers. At first I acted as though I found it very funny something had befallen her because I was mad that she had called me ridiculous on the last night we were together. Later, I was sorry.

"I loved her too much" is what I explained to her friends whenever I saw them.

"You barely knew her," is what they'd answer. "She only bought drugs from you." Yet I'd been with no one since, and so driving by the college girls seemed almost like old times.

"Let's go back once more," I had suggested to my friends. It was then that we ran out of gas on the edge of the city in a neighborhood they'd begun to revitalize. Although it was still known as Germantown, it had been done over to look like a Cape Cod village. There was a boardwalk for all the stores and a retirement home which had a giant windmill in its parking lot. But garbage scows came down the river every morning without exception spilling dead fish and squid, and sea gulls wheeled viciously screaming at any of the old people who dared show themselves. The whole area had become deserted.

"Ain't this some shit," I said to the passenger, who was streetnamed St. John and who'd remained inside the car with me. He didn't answer but got out and climbed in the back seat and fumbled around for a minute and then leaned over showing me a gun held in fingers near as fully webbed as a duck's. It was from a birth problem which also caused him to have no nose to speak of and had once led to him being nicknamed Fish-Boy. That was when he first came around. Now he was completely covered in tattoos in the form of religious memorabilia.

"We were," he pointed out, "planning on making some moves today."

At first I wasn't sure what he meant. This all took place in July in 1976 just before everything got real bad, and people were already being shot every day. "Whoa," I told him, trying to remember a pool debt or something similar between us; only it wasn't that at all, but instead turned out to be a plan they wanted me in on to get back some money of theirs which had been ripped off.

"We were supposed to buy a pound," St. John explained.

"There were two guys, one stayed in the car and the other told us we could be right there waiting in front of the apartment building where we'd gone to get the dope . . . said, 'I'll be back in ten minutes.' . . . How it got told, the person holding this pound was supposed not to like anyone he didn't personally know in the apartment, okay? Guy said, 'Ten minutes tops; I'm doing this as a favor is all.'

"And what he did was, in the front door, and out the back."

It occurred to me then why nobody ever had much to do with St. John, how the way that they'd been ripped off was almost so stupid as to make them deserve it. . . . Yet I was angry about being caught high and let go from work once again and happy enough being included in anyone's plans for the day. We didn't say anything for a minute, watching the seagulls instead. The driver had gone down to the river's edge and was throwing rocks at them.

"So," St. John finally asked. "you in; or out?"

It wasn't until we were all the way into a different neighborhood that I remembered the brand new car we had abandoned unlocked by the river.

"Oh that," the driver said, "we don't know who that belongs to."

St. John stopped us across from a tenement which

was really a hotel. "Here we are," he said. I looked around. It was a place like any other. The building's sign was mostly fallen in. Above it there were a number of windows and then the sky which seemed to turn and turn. "Why is everything turquoise," I asked. Several of the adjacent properties had been painted that color.

"You keep the gun," St. John said to me, "your experience will spell the difference.

"I'm going to wait out here," he said, "to warn you or in case any of them should escape."

"How many are there going to be," I cried, alarmed, "I thought there were only two."

"There are, there are," he said.

The driver and I walked into the lobby of the hotel. An old woman was asleep behind the counter and several winos were resting in chairs where the sun patched through the filthy front window. A parrot hung in a cage beside the window and I couldn't tell if it were a stuffed one or not. There appeared to be cigarette burns in several places on its fur and though either it or the old woman had made a noise of some sort when we first entered no one now moved or gave any sign they had done so in quite some while. All in all it seemed a poor choice of places in which to rob someone and I told the driver so even as we crept past the front desk and up to the third story landing where we stood one on each side of a door like they do in the movies. I had the gun out.

"Hit it," I told the driver.

"Hit it?"

"You know, the door."

"That won't work," he said, "why can't I just knock?"

"Okay," I conceded, embarrassed and disappointed.

When the door opened we rushed in in a flurry. I was pointing the gun everywhere. "Not at me," the driver warned. He'd pushed the man who answered the door down on the carpeting. A second man, dressed in pajamas, sat by a couch near one of the windows. He was rolling a joint. "Don't," this man said. "Just . . . please, don't."

"Motherfuckers," I told them.

The driver got up grinning holding the first man. "How's it feel," the driver asked looking from the one he held to the other. They appeared puzzled. "Reno Park," he reminded them, "last March—you did the apartment scam on us."

The man in the pajamas very carefully set the joint he was rolling in an ashtray on the arm of his chair. "Check this out," he said. "Look at us, okay? Really, really, look." He held his hands up in a gesture of resignation. "I don't know who you think we are, but we aren't. . . . And we don't know you at all."

DON JUDSON

Now it was the driver's turn to appear puzzled. He studied their faces. I could tell things were beginning to go wrong.

"Shit on that," I whispered to him and then pulled the man he'd been holding to stand in front of me. I showed the gun around to him some more. "What do you think," I asked this man.

"Oh God," he said.

"Because that's what I want to know."

"Oh God," he said.

"You ripped us the fuck off," I told him forgetting I had not been there to begin with for one thing, nor was it my money for the other. But nobody noticed and it didn't seem they could say anything at all anyway. I imagined that maybe I should make the victims go in the back room or at least tie them up, but it being my first robbery I was unsure. After a minute, I decided to break something. There was a glass-top table in front me and as I reached down to smash at one corner of it with the gun I swore again and then the glass cracked and the gun went off at the same moment the man in the pajamas sat back hard against his chair. "Oh shit," he whimpered. "Gerry. They shot me."

Both of them began to sob.

When I looked over the driver had tears in his eyes as well.

BIRD-SELF ACCUMULATED

"Damn," I swore. I went to the window. St. John was staring toward where I stood and we waved to each other and he crossed the street and I could see him come along past the steps to enter the lobby and a minute later he was knocking at the door.

"That's not necessary," I called out.

He came in and smiled at everyone.

"What's going on," he asked.

"I shot one of the victims.

"By mistake," I added, nodding to the man who sat holding himself at the shoulder. He and St. John considered each other for a moment and then St. John took the gun, but there had only been one bullet to begin with so he gave it back and then went into the kitchen and returned with a knife and began to stab at the injured man. For the most part he missed.

"Stop it," the man told him.

Finally, St. John cut at the man's pajamas several times and stabbed him in the same shoulder I'd already shot, but the knife stuck there and broke off. "Is this the only one you have," St. John wailed, completely exasperated and holding up what remained of the blade. He had begun to tremble and turned wildly from one corner of the nearly empty apartment to another until he finally found a lamp with which to hit the man. "Help me," he called to us, but the driver already stood

DON JUDSON

partway out the door, ready to run, and I was right behind him. "I wish I'd stayed at my lousy job," I muttered, angry and frustrated by the way his plan had turned out.

"Just one minute," St. John begged us. He'd overturned the chair and gotten the shot and stabbed man to lie face down where he could work the lamp cord around his throat. "Only just hold him a second. He's almost dead."

But anyone could see that it was never going to work. With his crippled fingers and the blood which had gotten everywhere, St. John could not get the right hold on the cord. It kept slipping loose.

"They are the wrong people anyway," the driver warned him. "I don't think anyone even lives in this apartment."

"I know, and that's why we can't leave them to testify," St. John insisted.

By that time, out the window there was a siren and while it could have been for most anything there seemed to be some commotion from the first floor hallway, and then I thought I heard someone coming up the front stairs and so grabbed the driver by the arm and headed us toward the emergency exit.

"Do you think he's right about the witnesses," the driver worried, unsure of what to do.

BIRD-SELF ACCUMULATED

"No one was dying in the first place," I reasoned with him. "And beside that, I don't care."

Several years later I saw St. John in a county facility where I was awaiting trial though it had nothing to do with the crimes of that particular afternoon. At that time St. John was trying to get into a medical program with the psychiatrists at the jail and so each afternoon outside of the dispensary would strip off his shirt and speak wildly about himself. There were several baby palm trees planted on the walk of the dispensary, which was brand new and housed all the offices where free-world people worked. There were windows, though not toward the back where they kept a special lockup section, and sometimes caseworkers or secretaries would come to these windows and watch.

"Sinners," St. John cried to them. His chest was bluewhite and hairless and depicted scenes of Christ harrowing the Gate, or driving before Him on the temple steps, moneychangers.

"All of you," St. John warned anyone who'd listen, "dead in sin."

And on the yard during rec. he delayed baseball games claiming to see from the sky angels descend— and these angels spoke through him as well in tongues—or recalled parables in a voice not his own causing him to shake in some fit of passion among the players, mostly black Cubans who turned away and crossed themselves whenever he rushed among them until guards came strapping him once more to a liftchair and carrying from the field St. John to back rooms to beat or medicate or both beat and medicate him into a silence which lasted generally some two or three days. And all of it, the insanity, or what he claimed to possess him, could have been actual, but more likely had direct relation to courtroom strategies while also serving as a shield between St. John and other inmates who'd rumored his jacket to contain charges involving the touching and harm of a child in St. Petersburg Florida—this being a thing which could get you killed quick anywhere St. John was likely to do his time.

Now all of that is long past and although I can't name exactly what it was I'd been waiting trial for, I'm sure I've done the same or worse since, though of course never what St. John was rumored to have done; and while I claim no small understanding of how right and wrong might add up to or become tipped in the direction of what is desperate, I do realize there to be things in any life which must be paid for at one time or another. And yet I have no idea what might have happened to St. John or if he was among those perhaps too

BIRD-SELF ACCUMULATED

pure in whatever it is that drives them to ever have to pay. But I do recall that facility when he was there one morning after a brief, dry shower during which the sun remained out and the morning hot and then the sky after the rain, bruised thick in its distance, and backlit by occasional flashes of a storm which could not build. I saw St. John stand in an unreal bleached light before the prison fence which steamed, and the grass, and behind further still the fence, the road as well steaming so that he appeared to stand or rise just off and above the ground, his arms outstretched, fingers scaled like wings tipped before the light, and he reaching as if to bestow:

"Listen," he spoke out to us. "Listen."

COMERFORD

Comerford is living in a hole he's dug in the strip of woods which runs behind Tucker's Pond.

That's what Rat says.

We are out in front of the drugstore, speeding still from that afternoon. At first, cars, as if in timed interval, come up from the factory road.

The sound of their doors—then emptied cans of beer or bottles banging in the wind across the lot.

Later, we drag oildrums from the gas station. Rat stands before one and presses the lid of each eye closed. He throws a match into the paper and bits of trash. Behind him a stoplight sways and clicks; looking from the light across the empty street to the long-shuttered tenements and storefronts it seems possible to believe no one has ever lived here at all.

In May, people begin driving out onto the playground to shoot up. You can hear them puke for a while and

DON JUDSON

then the headlights of their cars ease once more between the backstop and the low fence at the spot where
Baby Gangster was killed last year.

Sometimes I lie alone in the dark of my roof,
watching.

But most nights I'm with the others, far outside the
city—playing, trying to get lost. We snort small white
diet pills or mescaline. There is always wine. The roads
outside the city are blacktop and cut across marsh and
into pine barrens and the towns up behind them along
the oceanfront. But then the towns end and there are
low hills, and fields where cows stand patiently among
the rocks, and the ocean can no longer be smelled at all.
In these places, villages once stood. Most are gone. Yet
just when it seems possible none might remain, there
will be a turn and past it an almost ruined church with a
grassy drive in which a number of cars sit, and the
church doors thrown open to the singing within; or,
some half dozen stores and a post office—around them,
several homes, and on the front porch of one, or in
the street under a single light, children, barefoot and
startled, look up from play. Staring quickly past the
church and from these children to the weathered and
sprawling homes, added piecemeal or left undone from
one generation to another, I think for a moment there
is something I recognize.

BIRD-SELF ACCUMULATED

Where the hell is this, someone laughs.

What the hell is this?

And then the village is behind us, its few stores and homes, and we are back in unlighted countryside. Never actually lost, or not truly or for long. The roads here generally move with a certain determination toward one or another of the three major interstates and we almost always end within hours headed back again to the city.

Once, Tato followed a back route into another state altogether and then crossed from it to a dirt road which ran for some distance until it became little more than a washed-out path—rockstrewn, deeply rutted and with sudden turns—the largest trees receding from the path's edge for tangled underbrush and stunt cut pine which slowly closed over the car, branches slapping its window: a closed-in tunnel, impossible to back out of and from which for quite some time there had been no turnaround.

"Like an ambush," that's what Clayton, a former soldier who'd already gone to the war and had been sent home with nerves, explained.

"Incoming," he suddenly screamed.

Tato shut the car down.

"Shit man," he said. "Jesus Christ, Clay."

All that could be heard was the car ticking off heat,

and Clayton's ragged breath. "I can't see one goddamn thing," he cried. "Not one."

And it was true. Although we had come to a break in the tree line, an immense weight of darkness heaved and pushed itself from every direction. There were no stars. The sky didn't even seem to start anywhere.

"Jungle dreams," Clayton whispered. "We have," he said, "stepped into some distance here."

Clayton of course had been speaking of the past, of war, and killing perhaps—though looking at him, these did not seem things he should've known about, nor were they ones which fit the moment; but once he'd calmed down, we found ourselves on the edge of a meadow, and leaving the car, reconnoitering Clayton named it, there occurred to me a sense of stepping somehow past what might have been real and into Clayton's dream of himself and the jungle—Tato, and me, and Rat, and Clayton as well, no more than shadows, and I felt that this dream could have been as actual a thing as any other and that we were in fact in a place that not one of us knew nor would be able to find our way back to again.

Later that night we went by the playground and stopped in its parking lot. The junkies were still there. They had pulled their cars into a circle edging the baseline, lights turned inward, and there was a commotion.

BIRD-SELF ACCUMULATED

Three or four were attempting to put something, a body or someone passed out, into the car of another. But the car's driver was angry. Finally, everyone gave up and dropped the unconscious person on the pitcher's mound and left.

"What do you think we should do," Tato asked.

No one said anything. After several minutes the car in which the others had been trying to put the body came back. Two people got out. They squatted over the man they'd left behind for a minute and then pulled his jacket off. Looking up at us one of them shrugged, "He's my cousin."

As they drove off this same man leaned out the window and told us—"I think he's dead, anyway."

A dragon (emerging)—delicate arms, childlike but a hand hooked into a claw pulling it from a banked storm of clouds.

The eyes—parrot bright in which two lines bisect: one red, one green.

Fire comes around the mouth.

The man who did it, a fat biker out of place in the well lit and neat shop on a Worcester side street, tried to push other, more ornate and expensive tattoos.

"Think carefully," he'd said.

Sometimes there are memories of a child standing at the top of basement stairs. This is in Shelburne. I'm not sure how, but the child slips, cutting his head badly on the exposed edge of the second step, and tumbling forward, lands at the bottom of the stairwell, unable to breathe. His father is furious seeing tears. Or embarrassed. In other memories, the father has pushed the child.

"Oh my God," mother screams.

The dragon in the tattoo pulls itself into some fixed and unspoken absolute.

Whatever doesn't kill you, etc.

By nine-thirty I am up and dressed. Outside, puddles have guttered into dips where the sidewalks are buckled, and the water there is sheeted with oil and a chalky dust which seems to hang as well in the air—a taste, tongue, lips. Not rain, but the idea of rain.

Good morning, I say.

Up and down the street is nearly deserted except for several children who play before the rubble of a burned-out storefront.

Two boys and a much smaller girl.

The boys wear matching crewcuts shaved nearly bald and there is something compulsive, nearly sexual in the play of tendon and muscle about the base of their

BIRD-SELF ACCUMULATED

skulls; they clamber into and out of open window frames.

I imagine them to be family—the older of the boys in charge—and that their mother, most likely asleep on a daybed with some man, is glad to be rid of them for a while. Happy for the quiet. Because that's how it is— some man—because it is never given to be one, and constant, the men holding themselves apart from the children, and apart as well from the women, so that they, the women, are *here,* and the children, and by noon will be seen on the front stoops and sidewalks, talking among themselves, laughing, but not the men. Who are strangers sleeping in still darkened backrooms, who come out perhaps for a moment during the late day, moving past the women as if on important business. . . . And only at night, they stop—but to work on cars and get high, the cars and men soon gone.

As these two will leave their sister.

There will be a soft, down beard above their top lip, and on their chin, and they will be young men dull and angry—

Bang, the larger of them says coming up now behind the girl, but is ignored. "Bang," he repeats—she squatting above the pavement, unaware, secreting bits of rock and string in her mouth, and so the boy forms with his thumb and forefinger a gun held to the base of her neck and tells her, "Hey," and this time she looks up, eyes flat yet surprised, about to cry. The skin of her arms and face is translucent, bonewhite, and run below with a maptrace of veins, and seeing by the dirt around her mouth what she's been doing, or perhaps only his interest turning elsewhere the boy grabs an arm and leads her, all three disappearing through the alley-mouth without a word.

At ten Margaret Gleevey pulls up in her battered gray Oldsmobile. The rest of the morning we drive from one neighborhood to another stopping at tenements where Margaret is owed rent money. I go in while she waits in the car. Margaret watches carefully. I am supposed to count the money out in front of her.

"How much there," she asks, "how much?"

Eventually she begins to tell me, as she does every week, about Ted Williams, the famous baseball player.

"He's been hiding next to my house," Margaret explains, "seeing me undress at night."

I glance over at her, from the corner of my eye: Margaret behind the wheel, bent misshapen. At a point just before the line of gray hair pulled back, there is a neat clear half-moon scar where a robber used a hammer and left her mostly dead in the hallway of one of her properties.

BIRD-SELF ACCUMULATED

"Hey," the robber had whispered, and when she turned he stepped to her from beneath the stairwell. It was after that she decided no longer to collect her own money. My deal is for free rent.

"Ted Williams lives in Florida," I tell her. "He fishes."

We go along like that. She explaining about Ted Williams and how there is something in his eyes and me wishing to be rid of her.

Just before a stop somewhere along Dexter Street the foresky goes dark, a flat slate green, and the air is pulled up into the sky; against it buildings stand out essential and drained of color, oddly weighted. Children hesitate in play before them, women at windows pull wash from lines. In lots the trash—a discarded couch, refrigerator, broken bits of glass, the frames of doors or windows—stands out as well, each singular against the absence, indrawn, waiting.

"Here it comes," Margaret says, and then the first drops of rain, heavy and measured; the wipers go on and around us everything breaks open once more.

Baby Gangster died just after my parents moved to the coast—actually, my father had been gone six months before he called for us. Settling in. Getting things ready.

DON JUDSON

A new life, he wrote. A fresh start.

Yet I sensed, even behind those hopeful words, the slamming of cupboard doors, deep, intaken breaths, and the long, angry silences that had always been his language of disapproval. Everywhere about my mother and I, even then, although a thousand miles distant and its imperative therefore muted, still, rose and fell, rose and fell—"You will"— in everything he said, and me wanting no more. During the best of times Father was a difficult and angry man. But he drank. There was violence and that was a thing which had caused my running away, or, on several occasions, being sent to the homes of various relatives while "things cooled out," and one time involved even the state and me being a ward in the Children's Center—and though there had been talk of a court trial that time, nothing came of it and after three months I was back home. My mother came to get me. I can remember several of the boys I knew watching us from a doorway as we walked out past the cluster of administration offices, and my mother, who was very pretty and who that day wore a pale blue dress and looked hopeful as a small child herself, glanced up and saw them, and smiled, and misunderstanding, called out telling them, "Say goodbye to your friend now. This is all over for him." But they only

BIRD-SELF ACCUMULATED

stared at her for a moment longer and turned and went back into their cottage.

The sky that day had been the color of sand and low clouds obscured several buildings around the rail yards in the distance beyond the Children's Center where the city began, and everything appeared stripped and cold. It was the beginning of winter. Within a week everything was to be covered in snow, but I couldn't know that and as my mother and I made our way toward the parking lot I did not think of such things but instead listened as she explained how everything in life was no more than one moment passing by into another and that a person only had to outlive the bad in order to leave it behind. "Do you understand, honey?" she stopped and asked, a vague smile pulling at the corner of her mouth. And while I did not truly know, I believed she was only trying to explain that things were to be different. I told her so, and she laughed outright, and when we got to the car it in fact was not the same battered Renault always borrowed when my family needed to get somewhere and a cab or the bus would not do. Instead it was an Oldsmobile, somber and large and black, and though it was not a new car or even very well kept she'd had it washed and shined and the inside vacuumed so that it smelled as if it might be just off the showroom floor, and she told me it was ours. "Your father," she said, "bought it last week."

I knew that it was supposed to soften me up.

After a minute—as if in afterthought, she added, "He's been in a program. For his drinking and such."

What else I remember was how our apartment—its mismatched furnishings: vinyl curtains, torn and taped over; battered chairs and stickleg tables; and on these mother's "treasures" . . . small cheap figurines bought off the counter at Woolworth's—how these had been arranged so as to appear almost cheerful when we got home.

"Welcome," Mother cried out, flinging the door wide for me.

And how all of it, the car, someone's fifty-dollar cast-off for sure, and the sad attempt to make our apartment other than it really was, at once brought in me a sense of pity, and shame, and hatred; because it could be no more than a joke, and nothing had really changed, so that when my father began drinking again—which he did soon enough—there was to be more trouble, eventually including, several years later, a gun and another man from the neighborhood. By then I felt, though only fourteen, almost grown myself and when I came home one night and found him on the couch with a pistol as if he'd had the thought of using it

BIRD-SELF ACCUMULATED

on himself, I realized that while there was little I could ever say in order to make any person's life better I wasn't interested in his anyway.

"I don't know what might happen from this," my father told me. But soon after he moved to a small city south of San Francisco, and although it is not a place I know or have ever seen, I picture it to be set against cliffs so steep that below them the ocean might appear helpless and without effect.

"I don't know," he said and then they were both gone, she, as I mentioned, just before Baby Gangster got shot.

And that, which neither felt nor seemed like dying because though blood was everywhere and pooled about my feet as I knelt and beneath his head and on his shirt, and I could see—but all of it calm—the shots and Baby Gangster, falling, trying to speak. Everyone else had run so I leaned over to him. "Dude?" I said.

I wanted to reach into his wallet to strip him of something.

"You're not losing anything," I told him, unable to become angry at either of us, or at the shooters who'd driven off leaving Baby Gangster to die.

"This is too easy," I said. And I thought then of my mother and how when I'd confronted her and told her that I would not go to the coast—that I would cut my father's throat, and hers too if need be—all of it had carried beyond what could find return.

"Fuck you," I'd said, and that had been a death.

But this . . . I leaned toward Baby Gangster, embarrassed that I should be alone with him. And although he tried to speak and my lips formed, I believe, his words as he said them, I could not understand.

It was just dark—low, thin clouds massed like formless gray sheets bleached white were set against the sky, and lights went on up and down the Avenue. I looked at Baby Gangster. He appeared ridiculous, so young—just a boy, shot as if he were a man.

"Pray," I told him, unable to think of anything else.

It is at a party that I see Comerford, trying to keep himself to the fringes as usual, and he is surprised when I talk to him and then offer my apartment as a place to stay until things can come together. While I make this offer I'm thinking of times when people have allowed me to sleep on a couch or extra bed for a week or two, and I'm imagining as well Comerford walking across the playground alone, past the basketball courts and down into the woods, picking—how?—the exact spot he'll dig for himself a place to sleep and live.

BIRD-SELF ACCUMULATED

"Don't worry, man," I tell him when I notice the uncertainty in Comerford's face, "it's no problem."

Yet when he shows up the next night I don't recognize him at all for a moment. I have been smoking PCP with several girls from the neighborhood. One of these girls is short and has large breasts and has just been released from a hospital or escaped and does not want to return. She still wears a hospital identification bracelet and a paper gown which keeps falling open at its back.

"Oh shit," she has been saying to a second, taller, girl all night long. This taller girl is dressed completely in black and has painted her fingernails purple. One time I find myself in the kitchen, unsure why, and the tall girl comes in and we kiss, but when Comerford knocks everyone is once again in the living room watching a movie about a man marooned in outerspace.

I walk to the door and stare out at Comerford, his hair is luminous and damp. Behind him, in the street, is a pale blue Chrysler Imperial, its engine running. "Oh," I say after a minute and let him in.

Past the final rowhouse: several cut stone buildings and the two stripmalls which form an arc of light at the point

where they meet, and from one store Margaret emerges
and shuffles down an alley and out through the parking
lot of a Cambodian bar lit up as if this were another
country and then along a deserted street past the old
stockyards. The night hot, a pale thin strip of moon
hung against the thick sky, that and an occasional street-
light and the distant sound of traffic, and Margaret
makes her way finally through all of this to an unused
railway tunnel where legless veterans and insane people
no longer wanting shelters have built a city of cardboard
and tin.

Just inside the tunnel she disappears.

"Margaret," I would like to call out. But she would
never answer now.

There are fires in barrels back around the tunnel
wall, and the rest is darkness and voices which whisper
and nothing else until a face, white and ghastly, leans
up from the dark as if from nowhere and snaps its teeth
and is gone.

I look up. Beside a wall on a shoulder of blacktop grown
through with beachgrass and dry white flowers, Tato's
car is parked—doors thrown open—music from a tape
halted at a point in the air distinctly before us, then

BIRD-SELF ACCUMULATED

continuing, severed, apparently without form, and I think of children's gibberish, songs of one refrain sung over and again.

"What do *you* guess?" Cathead asks nodding at me and then pointing with his emptied can of beer.

Cathead believes the tornado will come, but the others remain less sure. All of it is of small interest. For a long moment I wonder what my mother, who in all her years of being in our city never once left the borders of her own neighborhood, would see here this morning. The same road and field and walls of course; the ocean she so well loved to collect in picture postcards. In our apartment, after *he* was gone, my mother turned what had been an extra, workroom, into "hers." There were knickknacks which had been stored in the cellar, lamps and spreads—the postcards. She had most on one large table in the center of the room. The shades were always drawn. It was cool and you could not hear the city outside.

"Where are we?" she would ask, smiling.

Her gesture encompassing in motion the tiny cut figures of rocks and trees, of animals and shepherds.

"Where?"

It was in this room I found her the week before we had planned to leave for California, coming to her, knowing I would not go, and I told her—what? The table was bumped. A figurine fell, and she drew back, stricken—perhaps in fear.

I felt myself grow around this woman.

"Stupid," I told her. "Stupid, stupid, stupid." And thought then I saw her clearly—the drawn-in white skin at her face and throat, the fragile play of tendon, a smell which was powder and heat. There was a moment, then my hands swept the rest of the figurines onto the floor.

"And if I did go," I said thinking of my father. "I'd cut him. Kill his ass. Do you hear me?"

In the end what could she do?

I was left in the "care" of an aunt I've not seen since.

This morning we have come here to get drunk and wait until the storm predicted last night touches down so that we can bodysurf the rocks at Beavertail. "Check it out," Cathead had told us, "the whole fucking situation will be out of control." And that had been the idea. Something out of control. A bit of danger.

Songs played out in our head.

Yet if I could stand outside I would see the three of them sitting on rocks in front of a cemetery for a community which no longer exists, and me just in back, and I would wonder about us not at all.

I spend less and less time with my friends. At night

BIRD-SELF ACCUMULATED

I avoid the places they meet. But I don't stay home where it has become impossible because of Comerford who stopped leaving first the apartment, and then his room, and finally his bed altogether.

In his room the shades are pulled close and there is a smell like moisture, cut open.

What are you doing anyway, I'd confront him when it started. I would move toward a window and then stop and face him, but he'd only shrug and ask me to turn on the televisions, there are two—one without picture and the other sound—at the foot of his bed.

What are you doing, I wanted to know, frightened for some reason, passing a hand through air gone heavy with the presence of him.

Very late some nights a dull blue flutter changes the shadows in his room and I hear a soft murmur of voices.

I dream.

And then get up and walk through the city. It is like this: the bars and strip joints shuttered down, doorways and windows empty, one or two men gathered around a couch in a vacant lot.

Sometimes, there is more.

Once I came right into a shooting.

It was very nearly morning. The man who had been shot sat slumped into the seat of a car. Although part of his head appeared to have been broken like strings of glass you could see that he was alive . . . still breathing, and each time he did a rattle of breath escaped his throat. I watched him like that for a minute knowing it would not go on for long. On the sidewalk in front of the shooting a beautiful Puerto Rican woman stood crying and pressing her hands together as if they were small animals which might escape. Several teenagers in gang colors talked softly to her.

It was a sound like pigeons cooing.

I wondered to myself who these people were. It seemed as if they might be my very own family and I wished to be included in their warm circle of grief, but they had not yet noticed me nor would they likely say a word when they did.

"Oh God. Oh, my dear God," the woman began to cry out. "Oh no. Please, please."

What power she had in that moment! It was as if the entire city had closed around her, and I, partially hidden, was unable to enter but only looking as she was urged toward the top step of a basement stair by the others. I could see: the car, a line of fire escapes, one or two lights which were on in windows, and it occurred to me then that there were no sirens, that no one else was coming out to look—I was alone with the four, and that not one of them would step forward because they thought it possible that whoever shot their friend might

BIRD-SELF ACCUMULATED

return; and without decision or knowing why, but perhaps understanding only that I *could,* I walked to the car and quickly reached inside its window, unsure even of what I was looking for, the thing I needed to take from the dying man, until I found it.

When I turned again, one of the pendejos, taller and more thickset than the others, was beginning across the walk for me. Behind him the beautiful woman had fallen silent.

"Motherfucker," the gangbanger called out as he worked a short length of pipe from inside his shirt.

Because it had started then I smiled and leaned back into the window and kissed his dying friend's face and came up with my mouth bloody and then showed to all of them what I'd already taken from the car. It was a wallet. I held it up in my hands and shook what little money was inside out onto the sidewalk.

"My friends," I said.

The one who had charged stopped short at the sight of my bloodied mouth and began watching as I carefully put the wallet in a back pocket. He fingered a cross at his neck and looked over to the others. No one moved. When I could see that nothing more might happen I stepped away from the car—hands out in a gesture of questioning—and slowly backed into the street and turned and hurried from them.

DON JUDSON

"*Cabron*," the thickset one called after me, "*usted arbrera en el infeirno.*"

The wallet is safekept under several shirts in the closet of my apartment. Inside are letters and cards and notes, and a picture as well, but not of the beautiful woman who cried on the sidewalk—although I've made up in my mind several stories about her and the dying man. Often, I see them together under trees in a park. They speak softly. This is the map I carry with me.

I would like to tell Cathead now that it is hurricanes—that a tornado, specific and of a particular path, has little to do with working the sea into any fury, and that none are likely to put down right along the coast to begin with.

I would like to tell him that, but it is useless, so I look where he gestures—to the Point upon which the compound with a rich family's four houses sits, and the sky there gone to a purple welt bruised yellow along its edge, and I tell him I guess so.

That it very well might be.

One leg raw against the sheet and mattress edge, and an arm thrown forward create a line from bed to window.

In the mirror I see him. His mouth as near, or

BIRD-SELF ACCUMULATED

memory—a voice which enters my throat—I feed him bits of bread.

For one moment smell what he must smell. (In this room, burning sap and overripened fruit.)

It is the same earth—houses, sidewalks, a smell of moisture, cut open. The same city.

In mid-August I decide to leave. To get away from the neighborhood. Disappear.

My way of going is through a job of night fireman at a children's psychiatric hospital which gives room and board. The hospital itself is a three-story red brick building. Its driveway curves through a stand of elms whose leaves are purple and throw shade on either side of a series of well-kept lawns.

"No one else knows," I tell Margaret as if there might be some bond between us other than indifference.

Outside her window women come to the head of an alley. They raise their hands to their lips and call children home.

"Shadows. Life. God's mouth," she directs these women.

I ignore her and point out that I will be at least twenty minutes from downtown. And then, although I don't believe it myself, I tell her Comerford will take over the rent collections.

"He wants the same deal," I say, "as if it were still me."

In the hospital I lie on a bed in a large square room, along a corridor filled with the offices of doctors and social workers. I memorize escape routes. They have been posted on a mirror above my sink.

Stay calm, is rule number one.

Make sure the children remain together during evacuation.

There are blue arrows and lines along which I can follow a path to safety. The children, most of whom have gone so violent toward their own selves that they must wear an elaborate getup of headgear and thumbless gloves twenty-four hours a day, would not be interested in these charts.

At night I dream of fires.

The security guard, night nurse, and myself stand on a front lawn. We have saved ourselves only. I can hear the children. They burn like empty walls.

I get up and piss down the sink drain.

Although it is nearly five in the afternoon, there are people in conference just outside my door. I stand qui-

BIRD-SELF ACCUMULATED

etly for a minute and then wet a cloth to put over my face against the heat and sun.

When I wake again the doctors and social workers have gone for the day.

I walk to the bathroom where there is a shower.

Back in my room I smoke cigarette after cigarette.

On Wednesdays, which is my only night off, I walk to a stripmall where I can eat pizza and drink beer with people I have never seen before. I sit with them, smiling—at strangers, at waitresses—and think about everyone back in the city who must wonder how or why I have vanished. Rat. Tato. The rest of them.

There is also a movie theater in the mall and I sometimes go to it.

Always, I'm back in my room by midnight.

"Checking in," I tell the security guard who mostly uses a tiny office just inside the hallway where there is a television and where he can safely eat Percodans, but sometimes I must go looking for him. Once he was out by his car in the parking lot.

"Look," he said.

The sky had been filled by lights falling across it.

"Happens every eighty years or so. Something to do with a comet." He handed me a joint half smoked down and we finished it and stood staring at the sky but I could tell they were not shooting stars at all, only jets and attack helicopters from the army base.

"Can you believe it?" he asked me.

Later that same night I woke to a terrible sound. I thought it was an alarm and could barely breathe. But it turned out to be the security guard calling to say that someone wanted to speak with me. The hospital has an old-fashioned A-board phone system. I waited. There was an audible hiss and crackling sound and then Margaret came on the line. She was speaking under her breath.

"He's right outside," she said.

"Who?" I asked although I already understood her to mean Ted Williams.

"He followed me again."

"You sound far away," I said. "Why'd you call?"

I raised up to stub a cigarette out in an ashtray I keep on the sill of my window. The lights had stopped in the sky, and beyond a knot of black I knew to be woods falling off to marsh and silt land were now visible the first faint signs of the interstate and the refineries which rise above the bay at the city's edge.

"I know where you go," I spoke into the phone, thinking of the deserted railway tunnel, of Margaret

BIRD-SELF ACCUMULATED

offering her withered tit to be palmed by filthy hands, in dreams of what?

"I saw—" Whispered, suddenly angry, wanting her to be afraid, but unsure of what had been actual and what not.

"Oh boy," she laughed back. "Yes yes yes—" then, "Wait."

The phone was dropped and I could hear her in the background—small, rustling noises. It went on for several minutes.

"Did you forget me?" I shouted.

But she'd come back on again. "It's all right," Margaret breathed.

"He's gone. . . . Okay. Listen. Do you remember your friend, Comerford?"

I said nothing.

"The rents I collect myself. He's been all the time right there in that room. There was a smell. The neighbors thought: he's dead.

"But he was just there in that room.

"The electricity was turned off, only he found a way to get it back. I had the water shut down. I saw him. I went to a window. 'Come out,' I told him. 'Please; can you hear me?'

"I told him, I said: 'now you must leave,' but he's

right there still today. I have to get a priest, or someone. . . . And *you* — I need you to help."

I begin to break into people's houses. Not to steal anything. Just to walk through where they belong. The first are in the Highlands, set off like tiny jeweled parks. It is a place of little worry. The sound of traffic from the boulevard one street below is no more than a whisper.

Then in neighborhoods closer by the hospital.

I believe that there is no place that does not see you.

Once, an old woman stepped right from the center of a miraculous light—she was only getting off a bus but it seemed like a miracle at the time, and I decided to follow her. She went into a section of streets filled with brown and cream duplexes.

She walked with small tidy steps as if each one were an allotment and did not look up or to the side even when I passed her several times close by, doubling back, trying to make her see me. I imagine that was a thing she'd learned, not seeing, but if a person were bent on some harm what good would it do her?

None at all, I can tell you that.

When the old woman started up to one of the duplexes no different than any of the others, I stepped back into the shadow of a building across the street.

BIRD-SELF ACCUMULATED

After a minute a light went on in her kitchen and I was surprised to see a man sat there. He'd been waiting in the dark. The man was bent forward, his chest against a peeling metal table, and there was a growth on his neck. It looked like four short fingers twined together. It was white and bobbed up and down each time the man moved his head. Which he did constantly. Like one of those plastic dogs in a car's back window. Something was very wrong with this man but I couldn't tell you what. Only another person like himself waiting in the dark would be able to understand such a problem. The woman fed him and then they sat together at the table not seeming to speak. Finally the man got up and shuffled over to the window. For a moment I believed he was looking out at me, and, startled, I moved back against the building, but he was only standing there thinking about whatever it was that was killing him.

What can a man like that tell himself each morning when he wakes up!

I began imagining myself in their home at a time when they were out, touching his hairbrush and comb, the brittle paper feel of her underthings. I was overcome by a sense of the quiet, the private quality of silence they must have owned and I wanted to end all of that.

The next week I go back to the apartment, early,

carrying groceries in brown bags which I fold and stack neatly inside on a counter once I've popped the front door. All that's needed is a drivers' license. The rooms of the apartment are close. Dark and without air. They are weighted with objects. Cheap prints and cutouts from magazines have been framed and hung on the walls which are white up high and stained and darkened along their base. I find half-filled glasses of water everywhere. China dogs, and dolls made of straw and bedecked with bright colored ribbons and pieces of cloth. In one drawer, photographs of a beautiful girl, many of them black and white, curling along an edge, placed carefully between cloth and showing over and again the same or similar scene. Rolls of dimes and quarters set on flowered porcelain butter dishes.

Out of time. That's how it feels, and me as well . . . removed, passing, gone.

Just before five I draw a hot bath and climb in with a bottle of wine and four Valium blue tens.

I lay out candles in each room. Put pictures from the wallet of the man shot sitting in his car around on mantles and a television and dresser top. At some point after deciding to get some food I find myself in one of the back rooms on a bed, an inception of the girl from the photographs . . . imagined, watching for signs.

This is you — I whisper.

BIRD-SELF ACCUMULATED

And, Us together—at the very moment I accept the old woman's small, neat, footfall to which I've given birth begin up the back entrance. But I remain frozen until there could be the sound of a key in its lock, and then, very aware and with a careful motion, take a heavy glass bookend and step quickly with it behind a curtain.

How often have I believed before or since that a particular time and place of some understanding had come, that I am into something so real that it cannot be taken back? I can remember waiting   for the woman

   for *her*.

How if I leaned forward, through a crack between the curtain and a wall abutment, I would see my own reflection in a dresser mirror. The thinnest line of body from waist to chest; the doorstop held slightly to the side before a shoulder—face halved and my right eye peering fully from the curtain's edge.

Can you believe me when I say that this was both me and not?

And that when I close my eyes now, here, what I find at night is no more than this: Comerford, his fingers working into the earth's fleshy knots, digging, with small animal patience.

PART II

What Holgate remembers:

Across Avenue B a guy stepping from an illegally parked Cadillac and beginning to walk toward him and BabyBoy. The guy wore a loose-fitting silk sports jacket. His shoes, in the sun, appeared almost purple.

What else?

BabyBoy standing. He'd stood and reached over his shoulder and touched one of the bags of cocaine arranged on the ledge—there were four of them, one ounce each, in clear plastic sandwich bags and they were not really hidden, but only laid out of sight along the inside lip of the window in front of Friends Social Club.

And?

The sun.

How the sun had felt.

The day so close it seemed as if it were being drawn through asphalt. As if somewhere just out of sight the city were burning and burning. . . .

This was up in Five Points. The guy was not supposed to get out of his car. He was supposed to only drive over and ask. That was it. Except now he'd been right there in front of Holgate and BabyBoy shivering slightly in the heat. The guy had looked to be maybe forty years old. There were black smudges on his forehead. His eyes busted out like Coke bottles.

"Hey kid," he'd asked, "you got a gun?"

Holgate remembers choosing not to understand this question. Of thinking in anger how he and BabyBoy had worked the corner for one month now, until that moment nickel and dime only, true enough, but had worked it nonetheless selling dope for one of the most feared men in the city. Plus, since before he was grown, BabyBoy being talked of as crazy. They did not believe that anyone would fuck with them.

Holgate had not thought it possible.

Someone from outside the neighborhood, an Italian, is coming with the money—that's what they'd been told. Wait for a guy.

For two hours they'd waited.

Now the guy showed—eyes whacked, and hair looking like it had just been dyed with something cheap, running in black streaks down onto his forehead—and wanted to ask such a question.

BIRD-SELF ACCUMULATED

"A gun, kid," he'd repeated, speaking up cheerfully as if requesting the time—"I asked you got a gun."

In that moment Holgate had understood, he'd seen in his mind the Caddie, recalled it driving by several times earlier, each time slowing and nearly stopping at the end of the street. He'd seen in one moment and had known then what was coming, as well as what he had to do, not thinking really, his body instead telling him, jerking back and immediately to the left. But the guy's hand had already come around from underneath his jacket and brought the barrel of a sawed-off shotgun across Holgate's forehead.

"Goddamn," Holgate had told the guy, "look what you done here."

He'd tried to stand but had been hit again, causing his knees to go out.

Holgate remembers all of this. He is sitting in the office of Centeio, the man he sells dope for. Both he and BabyBoy, who's waiting in the hallway, have been brought here by Centeio's enforcer and bodyguard, Lyle. Centeio would like to know what happened. "Tell me," he says. "Tell me what you remember."

There are cheap catgut stitches put into Holgate's face by the old abortionist who handles such things. He can feel them burn in the skin of his forehead whenever he stiffens against the ache which has begun there. The robbery itself had taken place no more than three hours before. A robbery, as Centeio has reminded him, of over two thousand dollars worth of *his* cocaine.

And BabyBoy. Centeio would like to know about BabyBoy. If he ran. "Because, a man run," Centeio explains, "I suspect that man of treacherous intent. It mean he might of set up the robbery his own self. . . . Maybe, maybe not. But, at best, a man run, he got no heart. That man leavin' *my* shit to be taken.

"Either way, example's gonna be set."

It is very dark in the room. Holgate looks toward the window, tightly shuttered, and then back in the direction of Centeio's voice. He thinks of how Lyle had brought him and BabyBoy, just several minutes earlier, to the office; and how he'd stopped BabyBoy outside the door and pointed him coldly to a chair. It seems to have been decided that he, unwounded, is not worth anyone's breath. Holgate considers this and finds himself unsurprised that his friend's life will be decided so cheaply.

"You positive," Centeio demands. "You sure he ain't run."

"Yeah," Holgate lies. "I'm sure."

There is silence. Centeio then very deliberately turns on a lamp. "Okay," he breathes softly. "Okay.

BIRD-SELF ACCUMULATED

Then tell me this. Tell me the one thing I ask of all people been working for me?" He stares hard at Holgate. Centeio is a man as notorious as Icy-John Dee ever was, yet Holgate feels no need to give an opinion. He knows full well that formerly the one thing asked was never to hassle a customer, but he also realizes this rule is about to be added onto right there as if the added on had always been the only thing in existence.

"I don't know," Holgate tells him.

With a great sigh, Centeio sits back, almost delicate despite his bulk, and tents both hands behind his head. "Robbery," he whispers. "Don't let no bitch rob you is what I say and say." After a minute he opens a drawer and carefully places a .45 caliber handgun on the desk's edge in front of Holgate. "This insurance number one," he breathes. "And that," gesturing with a soft flourish toward Lyle, "that will be insurance number two."

*   *   *   *

He came first in a smallish van, its windows set over with a steel mesh like the state bus which had dropped him there three years before, but now he came alone, sitting freelegged on the bolted wooden bench, trying to force his thoughts into some shape through which he might later recall a fixed point of understanding; yet

DON JUDSON

could not, noting instead only the bench, the shape of the wheelwell, and smell of the cigar of the cop up front. In none of these what he'd seen, but themselves alone—so that he, passing down the thin backroad where trailers of prison guards sat off in the heat behind anonymous motels, the trailer's yards boxlike and measured by triple strands of fence wire, could find little meaning when he most nearly needed it, passing too some several runoff ponds beside which the trees thinned and birds of an exact white were seen set against the sky (each imprinted against it as a single, perfect letter). And in these as well unable to find the idea he wanted, seeing instead *this is* . . . . Crossing two or more sets of railroad tracks and then intersections and a town's edge to pull up finally before its bus terminal where, uncuffed and possessed of one hundred dollars and a ticket as a goodbye from the state, he found all of what he'd imagined was lost and it was no more than him, standing in a strange town and waiting to go home.

Perhaps an hour outside the city they pulled into a large parking lot. At one end were bathrooms and some telephones and vending machines. He threw water on

BIRD-SELF ACCUMULATED

his face and hair and then stood outside. Everything was shadowed beneath endless rows of arc lights.

On the Greyhound he'd tried to read a newspaper but felt suspect. They'd gone past nondescript, weathered towns which came up from nowhere and then just as quickly were swallowed by hills and farmland. The towns all looked the same. Grassy commons with one or two statues and a fake cannon. Some benches. A church and several stores. Then an outlying fringe of stately homes, well lit and silent and where he saw no one save once a woman on a front porch. The woman had been of an indeterminate age and was skinny and wore an old blue sweater. Behind her, the windows of her house had been boarded over. Holgate had turned at that and it seemed as if the woman might wave, but she only reached for something in the darkness of the porch.

Later, clouds came down into the night. And stars just above and around them. They sat like small, hungry animals.

From eight o'clock to midnight he found a job washing dishes at the millworks in a railroad diner which had two rooms built onto it. When his shift ended he would neatly fold one of the four white aprons he'd been assigned and lay it on a pile in the washroom and then take off his cheap rubber boots and set them beneath a coatrack by the back door. The old man who worked through breakfast would already be at the machine, a cigarette, usually unlit, dangling cocked from one corner of his mouth.

"My friend," the old man always greeted him.

The diner, by twelve thirty, was between shifts of customers as well—those from mid-town, the theater-ticket affluent looking to balance their night with a taste of "atmosphere" would be gone or soon leaving; and the cops and hollowed out drinkers were some hours still from their regular rounds—so Holgate would write himself a ticket and then sit, elbows on either side of an oblong plate of hash and eggs, listening to the talk of those few holdovers or early arrivals who sat scattered around him. After, he walked the city until dawn. He'd go, as he had years before, up to the Tenderloin where the parks were and wander their paths, going down into darkness by the boathouse at Gramercy to sweat the dealers on benches by the lakeside carousel, and the whores and their pimps stepping up from nowhere, and then back out onto the avenue once more sweating hard as well white boys and Latinos who showed off gang colors and stood leaning toward one another on corners, waiting.

BIRD-SELF ACCUMULATED

East Side Boyz, they said.

Fuck with me or mine, you got to die.

But it seemed he was invisible, or immune from harm. He always ended in the neighborhood of Five Points, cutting through the backway by the switchyard, the ties grassgrown now—bottles, and boxes of millboard, and condoms used or not beside the railtrack, the train cars themselves sunfaded, their lettering gone, *R&D* or *Union Pacific* an outline but no more; and then on the streets past espresso shops and social clubs where of a summer night Italians in shirtsleeves and smoking cheap cigars would sit on cardtable chairs ranged along the sidewalk while behind them younger men wolfish in suits of three-hundred-dollar silk waited nervously, their eyes never still—past these and the Chinese restaurants as well where he'd once bought for fifteen cents on Saturday mornings chow mein sandwiches, thick and hot and running over the edge of a hamburger roll wrapped in wax paper. All of that unchanged, and the music stores and the broken down theater which became, at varied times over the years, always shortlived, this business or that, and the pawnshops, and alleys where still slept streetdrunks on pieces of cardboard.

"O, most blessed holy Father," the drunks sometimes called out.

Holgate would buy coffee and a half dozen doughnuts in a just opened shop, the Crown, or Corner Deli, and go with them to his room where he'd sit reading himself to sleep. By afternoon he'd be up again, catching a bus downtown to theaters where kung fu movies played over and again endlessly. Sometimes watching for a short while and then walking once more, thinking to himself—*What am I doing here. Back?*—but in his mind saying in answer, no more than passing time. Just that, passing time. And on one such afternoon, underneath a sky blue and emptied of clouds, he'd walked down to the pavilion at Belle Point and found sitting atop a benchback, BabyBoy grinning as he rolled a joint.

"Mister H.," BabyBoy murmured simply.

Holgate looked around as if unsure for a moment of where he were and then shrugged and sat down on the stone side arm of the bench. "You never know. You just never fuckin' know."

"That's it," BabyBoy agreed. He damped down one end of the joint and found a match and tried several small hits, checking the paper after each one to see that it was burning evenly before he finally took a single, deep pull. "Oh yes," he whispered, exhaling, "the pause that refreshes.

"Indulge."

Holgate took the joint from him drawing on it with short tokes.

BIRD-SELF ACCUMULATED

"You been gone awhile," BabyBoy smiled. "Done some real gangster time."

"What about everyone else, where are they?"

"Like the song goes, 'If folks ain't dead or gone they must be in jail.' "

"Rat?"

"He was around. I don't know now."

"Clay?"

"Busted."

Holgate took another hit and held his breath carefully before letting out only a shadow of smoke. He cocked his head, surprised by the potency of the dope and shifted forward on the bench.

"But check us," BabyBoy told him reaching the joint from his hand. "Young, white, and true to life."

BabyBoy laughed at that.

"True to life," he repeated, and some of the old men who liked to drink wine and play chess on tables set along the pavilion's inside wall where there was shade and quiet and where they met each afternoon glanced up then at the sound of his voice, an intrusion, and BabyBoy, in turn and without feeling smiled at them––his face quickly a face through bad glass, his eyes just as quick gone dead, and lifting outward both arms in exaggerated beseechment stood to face them. "Old men," he said, "what's up?"

And they looked away.

Yet BabyBoy, ready to show off, was not willing to let it pass.

"There isn't any out to this, if I don't want," he warned them. "It's a situation, and you lost."

Only when the men would say nothing to further anger him, did BabyBoy finally sit down once again. But he wasn't done.

"Do you think I give a shit?" he asked loudly of no one.

BabyBoy had a handsome, stupid face. His hair had been cut up into a kind of fade which made him look like pictures of the old fighter Jack Dempsey. The Mannassa Mauler, Holgate remembered. BabyBoy was dark like him too. Dempsey had been small and quick, when he'd moved in on larger men he had bobbed and weaved below their punches. Holgate was not sure if this was the way BabyBoy would fight but he understood him to want nothing more than to hurt one of the men.

"Silly is what they are," he finally said turning to Holgate who listened for them to tell him something back, but the moment had passed and there would be no trouble. It was quiet enough that he could hear leaves blow across the pavilion floor. And he thought then that it was BabyBoy in fact who was silly and that what he had done, as had always been the way with him, though this time of no real consequence, served little reason, and suddenly uncomfortable, Holgate looked away to the large paved lot next to the pavilion where there were swing sets and a fountain and a long row of partially boarded-up concession stands. Several children tossed rocks at the stands with little apparent interest. Sun glinted off of a broken window and surrounded the children with light. They stood in it picking rocks from the ground, and as Holgate watched them he remembered how when he himself had been young, nine years old, and on Avenue B had been struck and thrown by the front bumper of a truck it was BabyBoy who'd first reached him. "Little Man," BabyBoy had spoken, "you are very much crazy." It was a game. Holgate and his friends would dare the cars, cutting in front of them and seeing who could come closest to being hit. They yeasted one another up trying to show out for the teenagers, such as BabyBoy, who watched and took bets. No one had ever come near to beating Holgate when one boy, new to the game and to the neighborhood, passed so close to a car on his first try that metal nicked up the tail of his shirt. Holgate had felt his position challenged. Truly, he understood, it could only be ignorance which had allowed the other boy such courage, and yet it didn't matter. Holgate had bent down and retied his shoes and waited for a minute, timing the cars from the walk and giving himself a half step less than he knew he needed. Still, Holgate had almost made it. It was a small panel truck and swerved toward instead of away from him and he'd watched it come and thought in his mind, *There, now,* when it hit. As if by the act of striking, the truck too became, like BabyBoy's voice urging above the others Holgate to go for it, in the moment of hitting, both truck and voice as if *they* were *him* and wanting what had come, and later, on a bed in a room with high bare windows, listening again to BabyBoy's voice, his face pushing past others, smiling, "You might want to start a retirement fund," and forcing into Holgate's hand money won on him from bets, so that this too became part of a story which held them loosely over the years. And Holgate understood that it was the story itself, told over and again—someone remembering, saying, I was there, I saw, thus gaining a memory of themselves, a point from which to measure—I was there; and the story over time becoming one piece of the neighborhood's mythology. At its center, Holgate's name linked to BabyBoy; it was this, living together within a particular moment, which joined them, and nothing more. Yet still, on occasion, as if he too be-

BIRD-SELF ACCUMULATED

lieved, BabyBoy liked to act the older brother to Holgate.

"Got to school you to the new shit—," he began now, satisfied he'd cowed the several old men, but Holgate was no longer listening. He concentrated his attention instead on the children and tried to frame in his mind through them a memory of what he had known in the second before the truck. On that day, everything had stopped: sound, the light which held just off a building's window—and in it, a young girl suspended coming in half step from a doorway. Around him all of it unreal, the city, the street—"There," Holgate had said, without choice, without struggle. Then being hit. And that too a kind of freedom. He tried to imagine it once again, and as he did Holgate watched the children, who had walked to the park's edge and crossed the avenue to a section of warehouses, chain linked and barred across their fronts for the most part on a Saturday afternoon, and the children went slowly past these as Holgate watched and then up an alley and out onto another street where they disappeared suddenly among the tenements as if the city had opened and without thought swallowed the children whole.

There, is what Holgate had said, as if he'd been waiting.

Now.

A wind came off and across Dexter Street picking up scraps of newspaper and small bits of stationery and debris from vacant lots and threw them around Holgate's feet and into alley mouths and against the building's fronts. Although it was a warm night he had on a blue, hooded sweatshirt as did BabyBoy. Holgate pulled at the cloth of his along the throat trying once more to loosen its binding. He swore softly. BabyBoy looked up and shook his head. In silence they made their way past a New York system restaurant, and a tobacco shop, one wall of which was a magazine rack with an immense, paint-specked mirror running from floor to ceiling behind it, and at the corner by the Portuguese liquor store they turned right onto Cowden and into the neighborhoods.

It was the sixteenth day of May.

It was the second month of his freedom.

It was the third night of the first week Holgate had begun living with Cheryl, who was crazy, yet who he wanted to live with; and it was, he knew, back at work, almost precisely the moment his boss would be firing him for missing consecutive shifts. But it didn't matter.

Halfway down the block, at number sixty-eight, BabyBoy halted, his feet shifting in place as he looked from left to right. "Where the flavor is," he said, as much a question as a statement.

BIRD-SELF ACCUMULATED

Holgate, without response, started up the building's drive toward a small bungalow which sat there among the tenements. He went around to its back. Somewhere from an apartment's open window off to the left several voices were raised in laughter. "I didn't say *the*," one rose above the rest, insistent: "What I said. I said *like*. Like the fucken thing."

The others washed over him once more.

Out in the street a car rattled by, speeding, and then was gone. Holgate ignored all of this. He focused on a single, exact point of yellow light left on above the door of the bungalow. He stood beneath it impatiently settling a stocking mask over his face and pulling the hood of his sweatshirt up and fastening its drawstrings. In his right hand was a fourteen inch baseball bat partially hollowed out and filled with lead solder. BabyBoy had the gun.

Holgate nodded to him and knocked twice—a space between each. He moved back into the shadows.

Almost immediately the door was swung open by a tall, dark-skinned man in green, children's sunglasses, his hair slicked elaborately up beneath a snap-brim hat. "Yeah," he began, but finding BabyBoy standing there—the hood and stocking mask, a gun held out from his shoulder, hesitated.

"What," he finally said; "you playin', right?"

Moths ticked by the socket lamp just above the man's head. They bumped past and into the room beyond, which appeared washed of color save a calendar on a far corner wall. Jesus on the calendar was offering before himself like a gift his blood-rimmed and shining heart. Holgate could see it. He saw that and the yellow light alone as he stepped onto the porch and swung the bat full across the bridge of the big man's nose, and then taking the bat in both hands shoved him back inside the room where three slightly older guys, one of them partially risen from his seat, were gathered around a cardtable. "Son of a bitch," the one who had half stood up swore, and BabyBoy, following close behind Holgate, brought the gun up and showed it to him. The man sat. He and the others looked carefully back down at the money and scattered cards before them.

"All right," BabyBoy breathed through his mouth. "Okay."

They were in a kitchen. Brightly lit. A second fold-out table was set up with cold cuts and plates of bread. Above it, the calendar hung from a strip of tape. Further off, on a ruined counter, a clock and several bottles of wine. A dented tin coffee pot. One or two cups. Pipes were capped off where the oven had once been.

It was a place they'd come to and that was all. Holgate tried to recognize it as such. He glanced down at

BIRD-SELF ACCUMULATED

the pistol in BabyBoy's hand and thought: You are our lawyer, our lover, our best friend. That's what he wanted. To understand something which could not help but be what it was. Which would insure the robbery and himself.

"This will be fine," he'd said over and again.

Yet, instead, the whole thing quickly became balanced on an edge in ways it wasn't supposed to go.

For one, BabyBoy began taking his time—unwilling, it seemed to move as they'd agreed, and after telling the men to put their belongings on the table, went looking for a radio set to be turned on.

"Lose the jewelry," he said. "Make a neat pile. Rings, then watches. . . ."

"Wallets last," he added.

Holgate had been able to smell the sweat come up in the room. He'd stepped around the man he had hit with the baseball bat and who was now leaned forward from his knees, bleeding face cupped against the floor as if in prayer, and then gathered everything into a cloth bag reached from the pouch at the front of his sweatshirt.

"That's it," He'd grunted. "Let's book."

But BabyBoy only backed partially into an adjoining room's doorway, found the radio and turned it on. "No. Let's see;" he said musingly, "how 'bout that idea?"

"The fuck, you crazy?" Holgate told him.

For a week or more they had planned, most afternoons at BabyBoy's, watching television and drinking quarts of Green Mountain.

"Profit pure and simple," BabyBoy would explain. "Difference being—" and here he'd lean forward tapping his knuckles against the television as if to capture attention from the images wavering there. "First off, the entire realm of cocaine—the takin' I mean, jumpin' off and all that shit got you busted? Informed by right here. Right here," his hand flattened against the curved screen. "Cowboy shit. Don't have to be that way though. Get someone else, which I have plans to in the future.

"But now. Now everythin' be at a slow pace. And that bein' how come the card games."

The air around BabyBoy's house always tasted like metal. It was because of the factories. The type right there and whatever it was on fire inside them. But they had a cooler chest and drank from it until long after dark.

"The card games," BabyBoy pointed out. "These we're talkin' about. These card games are not protected.

"Just like a gift," he'd smile.

Mostly, they never saw anyone. The neighborhood was blighted. People no longer lived there. Some Cape Verdians would come lean against the brick front of the

BIRD-SELF ACCUMULATED

factories and smoke during their break though, and one day, across the yard in what Holgate had thought to be an emptied building, he saw a woman in a lowcut evening dress come down a back stair and at the bottom step hesitate, unsteady in three-inch heels, reaching to brace her hand. Later, in bed as he fell asleep, Holgate had thought of this woman, and with her came another, a second memory he could not connect, an image or series of them run together—unfocused, there, then lost—but which made him understand her nonetheless, not a woman at all but a child made up to look as one.

She seemed now prophetic as if events could be tied one to another in ways he might not see at all.

"*Who, what?*" BabyBoy had asked him. "Stay on the program."

Which had been the idea of the robbery.

In, and out—that was the program. Quickness.

Holgate wanted to remind him. To make him see. He told BabyBoy, "Four minutes, they been spent. We already gone. Goodbye. Past tense. Out of here."

BabyBoy did not bother to answer. He walked idly toward a set of double windows. Pulled their shades. Peered carefully around them. "Yeah," he spoke, as much to himself as anyone. "How 'bout that; how 'bout we just wait here a minute."

Behind him, one of the men, the one on the floor,

seemed to be praying. *Our Father,* he began, almost a whisper. And *please,* or another word close to it repeated over and over. BabyBoy turned at that. There was a pause. The only sound, the radio. Its volume down soft.

The man spoke again.

BabyBoy took a step. "Lay still," he ordered though no one had moved. He ranged himself over the man.

"Goddamn," he muttered, absent some way from his own voice. "Just lay still."

The gun was straight down at the man's skull and for a second it was as if his head had come open. Was blown open before Holgate—unfolded slowly like a place of cold air, from *here* . . . and for a moment it was real. But then he understood even as he saw that nothing had actually yet happened, no one had been shot, and found himself grabbing the gun's barrel before it could, pulling BabyBoy around behind it—Holgate braced, waiting still for the sound of the pistol gone off, but it hadn't.

Here it is, he spoke in his mind. But pulling nonetheless.

Then they were outside. Running. It seemed to take forever.

They ran, as within the pistol shot.

Mist like fog came. The streets empty and street-

BIRD-SELF ACCUMULATED

lamps broken off—refracted, unsure. Holgate thought of a movie. A camera which panned from a distance.

The weight of blood in fingers.

It was exact, and unvaried.

He studied her where the blanket had come down. Small, hard muscle just below the skin. Up high above her shoulder a scar he had traced before with finger and tongue. He wanted again to touch her there, maybe to bring pain or comfort, reached to do so, but instead stood and went out to the street.

When he returned she was awake, a magazine open on the table in front of her.

He went into the bedroom.

"What, given a choice, might you be," she asked reading from the magazine, "a botanist or a car-repair person?"

He came back in and crossed to the kitchen and from the refrigerator took from a plate wrapped in foil a slice of meat and folded it over a square strip of cheese. On a bottom shelf he found one of several beers from the night before. He ate looking out the window. "Which is this one?" he asked.

Her face was slack and marked with a pattern of

fabric from the couch where she slept most every night. He could hear her in the dark. When storms came, lightning filled the apartment only at its edges, touched along one wall, and she would be there—moving slow, then watching, her breath still. "Fuck me," she would tell him.

He the woman.

Holding, still and outside.

Sometimes he forgot this house. Rooms high ceilinged. Weighted silver horses used as bookends. Dolls sat in corners of the bathroom. Sometimes he thought when climbing the stairwell that it would become curved and wide. Its banister mahogany. A painting, nearly as tall as himself, above a carpeted alcove. The lamp, and something else. But he could only guess at what it might be.

She was sweating now.

The windows closed.

"People only tell the truth," was the next example she read, "because they fear being caught.

"True or false?"

She smiled at that.

Once as a child he'd walked in on his mother in the bathroom. She was reaching behind. There was hair at the spot between her legs. Don't see, he told himself. Fingers become a lamp. Chips alone of paint whose

BIRD-SELF ACCUMULATED

walls worn smooth. These, fit only. No, no—oh no to stop; and his own voice,

Bitch, he said, you—

The windows closed. Rooms high ceilinged. He pulled a chair opposite her at the table.

"Which one," he asked quietly, "which test is this?"

The fourth game they took was on Elmwood Avenue. They came right in.

"Gentlemen," BabyBoy announced.

The players seemed bored, looking off to one side until, just as he and Holgate were about to leave, and unexpectedly, BabyBoy told them to kick their shoes off.

"Now," he ordered.

A man with <u>Vic</u> stenciled above the pocket of his shirt set both hands on the table. First left, then right. He shook his head.

"Maybe our pants you want off too?"

The other players watched, attentive. For a moment it became obvious that Vic had begun to weigh possibilities, but in the end he did no more than curse and turn away and kick his workboots to the center of the room. Inside was an envelope fat with money.

"Twenty-five hundred," Holgate counted with disbelief ten minutes later as he and BabyBoy crouched together in a toilet stall at the Kennedy Plaza station.

"Well, well. Dude must've had business tonight more than just cards."

Holgate held silent waiting for more, but when none came he let it lay. "Come on," he eventually answered, "let's get out of here."

They went up an enclosed stairway, stone walls covered heavily in gang graffiti. Darkness shadowed several buildings outside, yet businessmen late from work still waved down cabs or, newspapers tucked beneath arms, hurried toward a lone bus.

BabyBoy observed them with a smile. He appeared as dug in as the city itself.

"Who's better?" Holgate muttered. "Right?"

BabyBoy didn't respond. He ran the fingers of one hand through his hair.

At the far end of the promenade and across Westminster a number of bikers sat on the steps of an old Methodist church passing bottles of wine and waiting for full night. Holgate had decided long ago that whatever was coming had already happened and he was only one more person waiting to find out what it might be. "The people we're taking off," he asked, "the reason it works they're just neighborhood guys. . . .

"A game of cards."

BIRD-SELF ACCUMULATED

"So?"

"So; twenty-five hundred. So; how come you know, you understand? the money's in his shoe?"

BabyBoy lit a cigarette. "We're doin' good."

"Right. We're doin' good. What we need now, after tonight, we need a new line of business." Holgate stopped any answer which might be made: "Let me tell you this," he said, "let me explain—you are fuckin' up. You are fucking up now.

"Think about it."

BabyBoy glared back at him and then fired his cigarette into the gutter. A line of sparks rose up around it. "Shit," he swore. "Christ." He looked off over Holgate's shoulder. After a minute he smiled again. "Check it out." Two Oriental women were coming toward them. Their faces were composed and perfect. Both wore tight black skirts. Holgate shrugged and started away. "How's this," BabyBoy asked putting a hand out to his shoulder, "you wanna make a big deal—I didn't; how the fuck was I supposed to know? All I was doin' was I tried to make sure nobody'd follow us. No fucken mo-mo guineas runnin' down any road in their socks.

"Okay?"

Holgate shook free and stepped from the curb. The cars moving slowly. He eased between them.

BabyBoy trailed after him a few steps calling some-

DON JUDSON

thing about getting together on the next day, but Holgate only waved him off and crossed into a building which let him out opposite onto a pedestrian mall cobbled over and closed to traffic.

Here college students strolled along in knots of three or four, the women often holding hands. They were fresh and clean and sure of themselves in a way Holgate didn't understand at all. Streetlights designed to look like lamps from the nineteenth century had come up, and lights showed in the windows around him as well. He found himself going past a storefront now empty but where he had regularly come years before, at seven or eight, several dollars in pocket, to buy for himself some small toy—he remembered in particular a brightly colored top and how when its stem was pumped down into the body and released it would spin wildly with a great breaking out of noise and colored sparks—but moreso he recalled how each week after finding the exact treasure he wanted among the cheap rows of five and dime tables set out in the store's basement he'd make his way up the dusty stairwell, in three distinct tiers, to the main lobby and go with the money left over, always enough but just that—having known what could and could not be spent—to the lunchroom whose side window looked over the street where men hauled freight or produce up onto sidewalks with two-wheeled

BIRD-SELF ACCUMULATED

dollies in the time before the street had been closed off and there eat sandwiches grilled in butter and sip at vanilla cokes.

Waitresses hovered. They smelled of lavender powder and cigarettes and perfume. Their hair was pulled tight with stocking nets and tucked beneath paper caps. He watched from the corner of an eye whenever he found chance, imagining to hear as well as see the crisp rustling rise and fall of their breasts.

"Here he is," they'd sing to one another, glamorous and doomed, "our little gentleman."

Had he always gone alone? It seemed it'd been something done on Saturdays—his mother giving him money, and he by himself . . . but Holgate could not be sure if that was always the way.

He slowed, and feeling a vague sense of anticipation, looked around finding among those lining the mall's center an empty bench, and sat. Music came from speakers mounted outside a video store. Men and women lingered by racks of dresses and tables filled with scarves and shirts set up by the front doors of several shops. No one appeared to be in a hurry. There was a promise in the street's elegance and verve, yet across from Holgate, through the slip of a tiny alley, a man who looked to be dead lay sprawled on his side as if flung there from a great distance. The man's pants were pulled partway off and shit was smeared across his back. Holgate reached a pack of Kools from his pocket and lit one throwing the match into a concrete planter where several emptied pints of blackberry brandy lay already face down in the black dirt. They were surrounded by the shards of other bottles.

"For they shall inherit the earth," he said to himself, unsure exactly of who or what he meant by this. The dead man? Himself? He laughed and tried to replay the thought in his mind but there was no connection.

Two students, or so they appeared, came up the alley absorbed in discussion and nearly fell over the corpse. Both men jumped back and then eased forward cautiously again before one of them reached out and gingerly pushed the body back and forth with his foot. The dead man immediately swore and sat up, which caused the two to skitter to the front of the alley smiling uneasily. Holgate studied them trying to imagine their lives, asking himself what they would be made up of but could get no clear picture at all. He drifted from the attempt to a series of images running through his mind, none holding, until he saw the parking lot of a stripmall on the Cape sided by two roads which merged together at the lot's end.

Which town?

BIRD-SELF ACCUMULATED

He was unsure, and trying to name it saw a different road, narrow, its paving uneven—from one point a stand of scrub pine, how in the noonday they baked, and beyond them a thin slice of harbor, several boats put up outside a building with high doors. The smell of resin and salt flats. And there a shadow of small white bones pinned by the sun. Movement as if sound to gather—something.

The separation of hands, or, stirring toward need.

He could see the place now. A vacation years before. Holgate took a breath. He lowered and closed his eyes. There was a path to the water nearly overgrown, a green there of perfection almost angry. It took over tree limb and bush.

For a moment only that.

When he opened his eyes again the two students were emerging from a coffee shop. They held styrofoam cups. The one who had tried to rouse the wino peered into the open alley shaking his head, but then both became focused once more on whatever conversation they'd been having. Going back and forth they wandered toward Holgate's bench and settled at one end. Up close he could see that they were older. Teachers most likely; the university's buildings dotted the area.

DON JUDSON

"So, make me understand," one of them was insisting of the other, "Make me comprehend how you can say that at all."

In the city around them which could not be seen, women hung clothes off the rusted arms of fire escapes. They walked from room to room—their eyes blue, then gray, then white. Outside, the streets filled with men. Like insects, they twitched and rubbed.

"Make me understand," is all this one wanted.

Holgate settled back, comfortable with the same pull of anticipation tight at the edge of his knowing. It's the possibility, he thought; the principle of it.

There was over twelve hundred dollars in his pocket.

Nowhere he *had* to be.

A breeze worked along. He leaned toward it, glancing up when he caught a change in the pitch of the teachers' voices. They were standing, getting ready to leave. Holgate watched them pad by. Both wore slacks, and one a blue, the other a green tee-shirt.

Their faces were pale and adolescent.

He looked after them. The pale moon of skin, a breeze rising and dropping. Holgate felt drowsy.

He held still for several minutes, aware of nothing really beyond the holding itself, before he got up and started away from the mall.

BIRD-SELF ACCUMULATED

He walked slowly, stopping once at a bookstore. There was a bright neon sign in its window and inside were three stairs leading to a second doorway and the shelves of books.

Holgate went on, deciding not to go in—it was cool between the buildings, and quiet, and he went on and passed several narrow streets where business owners had stenciled their names in paint above stone archways, and then crossed up a nearly deserted boulevard. The boulevard ran in a straight line. It looked like a movie set waiting. Stoplights clicked. He paused, searching his pocket. The stoplights went green, yellow, red. He could hear them. There was no traffic at all. In a coffee shop across the way a man sat alone. On the table before him lay a book.

The man's features were shadowed and he appeared tired. He lowered his head toward the book as if in prayer.

Blessed or dearest Father.

The light on the man and the unopened pages became then: as an ocean. His mother by a window in a house before it.

Somewhere voices and the separation of hands.

Holgate put a cigarette to his mouth. He lit a match, but as he bent forward to it, hesitated. There was a sound, or a sense of movement at his back. Ducking low by instinct he stepped out toward the street and faced around to see a brindled mutt which looked to be a cross between a pitbull and some larger breed launch itself with such force against a cyclone fence just behind him that the dog turned itself sideways. Spittle flew from its massive jaws. Its eyes rolled back and it mouthed the webbing of the fence with the same dull instinct a shark might a piece of bait.

Holgate stepped further back. The fence, which surrounded a lot and which he'd not noticed before, was little more than waist high. He saw that the dog could get to him.

"Christ," he swore.

There was no place to run.

But in the moment of realizing that, and as suddenly as it had appeared, the dog was gone. Someone gave a low whistle and it trotted off toward the lot's far end where a trailer and several bulldozers could be made out as deeper shadows against the sky. Piping for water mains was stacked as well. A smell of tar and fresh laid dirt. His own fear. Holgate stood as if to memorize all of this, measuring against himself—listening to the dog's frantic breath, the scrabble of its purchase along the fence, and a deep, low, keening moan nearly from its throat. He tasted ammonia. Something metallic—

BIRD-SELF ACCUMULATED

muscle-cabled and blood. All of this, clearly edged, stood out between. Holgate watched the place where the dog had been. A mixture came of revulsion, and shame of being scared, and anger. He thought he might go find BabyBoy and get a gun and shoot this dog. He was in fact sure of doing just that and started in his mind back toward the mall, not taking a step in truth, but thinking himself about to . . . once, twice, before he changed his mind and sat down on the curb. He'd dropped his matches and he pulled them to him with his foot.

He looked around.

There was nothing to see.

At a far cross street a legless man on a cart sold pencils. A car pulled past him, and then a second. All around there were buildings as if rusted or bled from brick.

It felt as if there should be something else, but there wasn't.

The first story he told was about the *county jail*. That's how he said it. As if it were something important.

Okay?—he asked.

The story about three men who'd held down a

DON JUDSON

younger one on the cell block during a night and how they took turns on him.

The sound of it.

He tells this story in a bar. There had only been two people at the counter when she'd come in.

Beaner—one of them called out to her.

Who? She reached to find a cigarette. It was him and he'd been there with BabyBoy. Then BabyBoy left.

Cheryl—she explained—that's my real name. No more Beaner.

He moved down the bar next to her but it wasn't until he'd stood a second time to play a song on the jukebox that she saw how much older he'd become. She guessed that to be what jail did.

What was the song she used to sing?

About the boy who's taken some money.

The jail is old and runs for a full block past the edge of downtown. Sometimes when she was a little girl she walked there, following the riverbank up past the railway tracks with factories just off behind them. She could feel everywhere the reckless tension of the men inside.

Yes—he stopped her—okay, but you can never *really* know.

Later, when the band set up (and she'd noticed how

BIRD-SELF ACCUMULATED

drunk she was, how drunk they both were) they danced, slowly, clumsily, his hand at her back, whispering. . . .

He told her—You—and then began the stories; she recalls them about jail and prison. How he had come back.

Like the myth—he said—Ulysses descending.

For you—he told her.

It was probably as real as anything.

Yet when she is alone her daughters come. They come—and spread like fingers, fanned before a shadow and young women, the flash of white arm.

To him she tells, yes, but always seeing the story of jail and the young man raped, working loose later a piece of wire from a vent to sharpen in secret.

He, waiting until the three were asleep. Waiting for silence. Coming up on the largest of them.

He'd been trying for an eye—is what she'd listened to that day in the bar—but at the last minute? Because he couldn't look (but doing it anyway) he missed, driving the wire through a cheek where it must have hit bone, popping out then like a fish hook.

Exactly like.

Can you imagine?

She thinks it is no more than what all men see when they watch.

Alone, she calls and her daughters come covering a window and mirror in black cloth. Give *us* a story, the want of her.

The fat boy who owned the apartment had fingers like blood sausages without color. In fact, all of him resembled a dead man whose inside fluids have pooled and swelled except for how he was an albino. In compensation for this he wore a black dreadlock wig that looked to cost about four dollars and was the only hair on him at all.

"Ready here," he said.

Once or twice he'd nearly dropped the spoon. But now he had it. His little albino eyes were locked in concentration.

The fat boy's name was Elvin. He and the other people who belonged to the apartment, a woman and two men, had been shooting crystal meth and smoking heroin since the beginning of Friday afternoon three days before. That's what the little ratfaced one told BabyBoy and Holgate. They'd just run out of meth, he explained, and Elvin had found instead a dozen reds.

But now he insisted on cooking them up.

"The simple reason of not doing so," Ratface went on in an exaggerated voice, "is which it cannot be done."

BIRD-SELF ACCUMULATED

Elvin glared at him. "Don't tell me," he said, "don't tell me what I'm thinkin'. Don't even try."

Ratface shrugged.

"What I'm tellin' you is simple."

This time Elvin did not respond. He adjusted a lamp on the wall beside him. The rest of the room was mostly dark and had been decorated in dayglow posters of cartoon characters doing things you might not expect. In one Mickey Mouse had a giant erection. He'd bent a famous movie actress over a table. Cartoons were on the television as well. The volume seemed to be broken and was going up and down.

"We have obtained," Elvin announced over the passing sound of it, "lift off."

He shook out several matches he'd been holding beneath the spoon and drew the dope carefully through what appeared to be an already stained piece of cotton.

"All God's chillen," he smiled and although it took him several tries to find a vein—they were thick but seemed to roll beneath the needle—he eventually murmured softly and loosened the surgical tubing he'd tied off with.

Then began the slow pump.

As if in response, the television's sound had faded once again. On it someone's eyes were kind of exploding. They shot around from wall to wall.

Elvin's own eyes were closed. An amazing thing happened. The vein he'd hit formed a bubble like a tire about to blow, and as they all watched—it took no more than a second or two—the knot of vein expanded just beneath the skin and then burst sending a thin jet of blood three feet up the wall.

"Whack, bim, pop," Ratface canted in triumph. "You cannot cook reds."

Elvin let out a cry. He appeared to go into shock.

"Goddamn," he told them, "someone get a towel," but was already pushing away from the table himself. His wig loosened violently to one side and he hurried bentwaist toward the kitchen with the queer shuffling gait of a fat man, finger pressed to the crook of his arm as if protecting it from sight.

Ratface was smirking to himself. The other man just looked at the wall and blinked. Although this man was not wearing the same gray workshirt with his name stitched above its pocket, and his hair appeared to be combed in an entirely new way, Holgate had recognized him from the card game they'd robbed just the week before.

Vic.

Right. The one with the twenty-five hundred dollars.

BIRD-SELF ACCUMULATED

Damn, he'd thought walking into the apartment and spotting him. And looked over to warn BabyBoy. But BabyBoy had only smiled. He had suggested this as a place they might score some smoke cheap and since the moment they'd arrived that's all he'd done, smile.

Yet still it came slowly: not only was BabyBoy having fun, he'd *known*.

He'd of course known that day—about the money, where it was, and why; and he'd known this afternoon as well when they came exactly who might or might not be here.

Now he crossed and sat on the television with the same stupid smile for Ratface and Vic.

"Boy," he said. "Goddamn, right?"

They didn't seem too interested. He looked down between his legs at the television screen and then back up. Elvin could be heard banging around in the kitchen. BabyBoy listened for a minute and then seemed to attach a thought. Narrowing his eyes, he stared at Vic, puzzled.

"Hey, ain't you the guy? One who got robbed, the other day—the card game?"

Ratface and Vic glanced to one another. Vic sat up on the couch. He appeared suddenly to be someone waking from a sleep, pulling by force of will to ascertain once more his own body—which was large, and power-ful, but as of yet at a remove—sensing of course.

Within a breath he was there.

"It was on television you see this? The cartoons. Because I don't remember any particular thing being advertised."

BabyBoy kept smiling and stared down once more at the television like he was expecting it to be true that a whole story about Vic and his robbery was being told there. But all it showed was the cartoon man whose eyes had bugged around earlier about to be exploded by a stick of dynamite he held in his hand.

BabyBoy laughed. He began whispering to himself.

His mouth worked carefully. He had everyone's attention. It was as if he'd said: Watch, I'm going to show you a magic trick.

Or—Here it comes!

And it did.

"What," he finally wondered out loud. "What did you say to me?"

Elvin was already back in the room. He held a bloody paper towel to his arm and was looking in dismay at the gummed-up works on the floor behind the table. He started a noise low from his stomach like an opera woman but BabyBoy interrupted taking out his revolver pistol. It had been tucked beneath his shirt and

he slipped it out and stepped back and shot the television.

"What?" he asked Vic.

"Because I couldn't with the noise and all—I
couldn't hear." His teeth still showed reasonably yet in
some way pointed in the opposite way from the casual
tone in which he spoke. "Did you accuse? Did you say it
was me and my homeboy; did you say that?

"Us who robbed you?"

"Hold on now," Elvin tried to interject. It seemed
for a moment he might have a plan. He held the bloody
towel first toward BabyBoy and then the television.
"What we got—we need to regroup. Get some reality
on this situation.

"There's no need," he insisted, holding up a meaty
hand.

BabyBoy tried to shoot it.

"Boom!" he shouted after the gun had already gone
off missing the target altogether.

Everyone began moving at once. Elvin was gone
back toward his kitchen. Ratface and Vic jumped the
couch. The woman kind of fell from it or was pushed by
one of the others. She looked to be sleeping. Maybe she
was and had been all along. Holgate wondered at that.

He saw her to be dressed in plastic industrial straps
at each ankle.

This was unusual.

It made him wish to touch the woman like a younger sister, just reach the hair from her brow, but BabyBoy had begun filling the room. He just shot it all up. "Boom!" he continued to yell after each report faded, but when no one showed his face or gave him anything in particular to aim for, he finally became disgusted and went outside.

He and Holgate stood together in the yard.

"Still worried?" he asked. "Still think we're gonna have a problem?"

He shot out a window and then shot the door twice.

After that, he was out of bullets.

And I in cool bedclothes
dream those were nine years like summer
my hand   unbreathing
for the dark blessing.
Pray. . . .
The first time I came to men I also let them see an empty room. Eyes too cruel, as a young girl being widowed, hauling before rain. This is we are to be as stems. It was 1974, both babies gone, and my doing they said.

BIRD-SELF ACCUMULATED

Tied to this, women can have as well.
Was I to watch from the window
a man
as if a change in weather?
        —You were high, one accused.
At that moment I was able to read him and read him
from the end of the world.
        —Asleep, with the children left like that.
        —Stupid bitch, he said.
Yet everything hanging back between dream and
    waking
half blue and bluer
I in fact cannot remember or know what else to say
St. Ignatius, your doors open and close
yet inside the landscape we cannot know where we have
come;
our memory of older doorways
creating here the useless, backward looming
line which distinguishes it.
Noise remains delivered.
The dream of the Annunciation,
the bird that is the Holy Ghost.
It is here collected as the distant yellow houses.
God killed them both—
the light of the light of the blood inside each leaf.

DON JUDSON

With you before the theater:
The blacksleeved crowd
thinks only hours
but we are of whom the hill
unites
and now, the water.
It is a dream of the first sister
in which you wake to find yourself covered in white
sheets,
walls, and doors,
a fear of no words
of words falling
over and over.
Hold me tight and sing hymns.
She barefoot and sounding far. To be sent forth backward to walk the finer row. A world history prepared
in bends.

Holgate went back to the bookstore. It was a morning
a week later and it was hot, the sun still not full above
the buildings, but strong, and inside the bookstore were
ceiling fans and it felt cool and quiet.

He bought a copy of essays and a book of Spengler's
and one on philosophic structure. "Will that be all to-

day?" the woman at the counter asked. She smiled at him.

The mall had been swept, and a fine powder of dust was in the cracks of pavement where the pigeons fed, their throats gray and dull, and iridescent just at the moment of feeding. The dust was on the feet of the pigeons and in the air around them.

It was early, few businesses open. Holgate found an art supply store owned by the university and picked out a sketch pad and two boxes of charcoal pencils.

On this and other mornings radios had begun to play summer songs.

At first, Cheryl liked posing for him. She was high whenever she was awake anyway and didn't mind staying in one place for a period of time. Nights, she spent alone in the living room unable to sleep in their bed.

"It's a thing I'll get over," she insisted.

Holgate set a small table up at a corner wall of their apartment to give himself a place to study. He worked on several letters. *Dear mother,* they began, but he threw them away.

Written on a piece of paper above his desk: History as a necessary fiction.

There was an idea, a way he'd wanted things to be when he got out of prison.

DON JUDSON

"Okay now," he told himself each morning.

Arranged behind thoughts, an indication of shape— shadow unformed.

They were sitting around at Jackie Dino's. Holgate, JerryDog, Gamache, and BabyBoy. Jackie was there too. He was telling a story. "That time for the Roy Jones fight," was what he said to the others. Jackie had once been a middleweight boxer. Now he was mostly a junkie. "I was trainin' upstate," Jackie told them, "at Carlos Tee's place. Carlos runs marathons and he's pretty good. He had a doberman pinscher named Baron. I was runnin' up those hills and I was tired.

"Understand, I took a little taste every now and then.

"But Carlos, he was like a fucken machine—'Come on,' he'd say. 'Come on.' And here we were up in the hills and I look back and Baron is foamin' at the mouth. So Baron dies. And I told Carlos, 'Look, you just killed your dog. I'm outta here. I'm not runnin' up here . . . your dog just died.' That's the last day for up there.

"The idea was to keep me—you know? keep me away from everythin' but now I'm back in the city so forget it. The fight comes, and Jones—this guy was ready, no shit—in the fifth round I hit him with a left hook right at the belt. It was a punch I could feel all the

BIRD-SELF ACCUMULATED

way to my shoulder, and I looked over at the canvas
after the bell because I thought he must be goin' down.
But he just stared at me and said somethin' that had a
lot to do with my mother. Then he walked a straight
line back to his corner, and I knew.... I was outta
gas, right?

"After that he opened me up pretty good."

The room they were in was an office for the bar
Jackie managed and had in his name fronting for some
other people. It was private and dark and cool. Cases of
beer lined the walls. The back door had been left open,
and a nice breeze came in through its screen. Behind
the place was a dirt parking lot and a small pond.

"Opened me up good," Jackie said, and everyone
nodded in solemn agreement and looked off as if the
fight were taking place right before them, though in
fact it had been ten years since Jackie had fought at all
and he was an addict now and no one but him remembered the fight or Roy Jones in the least. Maybe Roy
Jones was a person who in his own life also worked his
way into running a bar. Which is a thing that often
seemed to happen with fighters—the journeymen anyway. The very good ones sometimes made too much
money too fast and got crazy and bought homes in
places like Florida and stocked them with video games
and beer and stayed drunk. Maybe that's what Roy

DON JUDSON

Jones did. Maybe Roy Jones was one of those. Who could say? He was just someone else who'd beaten up on Jackie.

Outside, in the near distance, a truck's brakes caught and then someone called out in Spanish, and another voice, in English, answered, though the voices did not sound angry, nor did the truck's stop seem anything more than measured and careful.

After that it was quiet for a moment and in the silence BabyBoy stretched both arms around the back of his chair and yawned. He glanced over at Holgate with a tight smile that was hard to read. An hour earlier they'd stood together on a lip of sand by the pond. Several rusting cars had been driven down there and left, and empty boxes were piled around and a refrigerator and parts of two or three more.

"Let me see the pistol," Holgate had asked.

They'd been having more words about where things were headed.

He could recall a beat of five or six seconds which had passed then, and the way BabyBoy's eyes remained hooded as Holgate had shaken five bullets out from their chambers, spun the cylinder on the one remaining, and cocked the pistol and held it out before him.

At first it had been like a dance. Holgate putting the gun to BabyBoy's forehead and BabyBoy turning his face slightly away to the left. Then with quick half step Holgate coming back around. Once, twice, and again until Holgate willed him at the pistol's end and it stopped—he dipping forward in unasked question, gun arm tensing and lifting. And then that too ended and he just held BabyBoy out there in front of him. How long they'd stood—the gun squarely to the face of BabyBoy who stared off impassively beyond it—he wasn't sure. He'd only known he'd become tired . . . of the sound of his voice, of BabyBoy's . . . all of it. Finally, he had taken the gun away and brought it up once more, pointing the mouth of the barrel this time to his own head and pulled the trigger, and when it clicked on an empty chamber he'd turned and tossed the gun into the pond.

"Okay?" he'd told BabyBoy.

"Fuck the gun; fuck you."

Now BabyBoy began a story. It was about someone disrespecting him in a restaurant or something. It was about nothing. BabyBoy most likely meant to make a point but Holgate was not interested. He went and stood by the screen door.

It was going to rain. The sky appeared to have been burnt and pulled back together. It would drift like ash to the dirt of the parking lot and rise again, bits of prayer.

Inside the room, JerryDog stood and went to the front and came back with five beers. The beer had been iced in the cooler chest. It sweated across his hands. Gamache lit a cigarette. He leaned back in his chair and then forward again and drank.

Just below everything, BabyBoy's voice.

Holgate saw the words form. Could hear them.

"**D**eliverance," she told him.

Not able to rest because not able to know.

They were chaste. Unwashed. Children together. He went for bagels from the corner, and hot coffee, and they sat beside one another on blankets which they lay across the narrow fire escape.

"To . . ." she said in honor.

The day had already come. The whitening of the east spreading over the west. Mourning doves warbling. These colors: a blue weight, whitecaps.

"All love," she told him, "doesn't end in tragedy."

He wished to get beneath the blanket but had in mind the stories about her father. "They all want to touch," she insisted, "put their hands inside.

"Can I trust you?"

One time at a coffeehouse there was a man they both knew just slightly and she moved her fingers along

BIRD-SELF ACCUMULATED

his cheek, telling him that he had lipstick there. Later, she was furious because he'd not responded. "He hates women," she decided. "What was he doing out there with those people anyway? He doesn't belong."

At night she dreamed sounds and cries. Could smell women up from the shower drains. Everything broken open.

The sun was up. As the morning wore on it would begin to climb and tick along the fire escape. "Like a pussy," she said, her eyes closed to it. "Will you eat the pussy, will you eat its blood?"

It was too hot to sleep. He went to movies all day and refused to leave. Sat in air conditioned restaurants— anything at all. One afternoon he rode the buses to the west side of the city. He walked around a little and then paid five dollars and went into a museum that had once been a private home. All of the museum's rooms opened onto an enclosed garden at its center. Holgate took his time looking into doorway after doorway. One entire room had been carved into a Medieval chapel. In it were cases of daggers and masks as well as several books made out of wood. Other rooms were filled with sketches and prints, and after a while he came to an alcove set off by itself. Two old men in uniforms smiled at Holgate, guards. There was a stone bench there, and above it and to either side several lights played on a painting of a woman from the fourteen hundreds posed, her figure appearing serene—head lowered slightly and hands folded against her lap. But the woman's face was different, the rest of the painting appeared washed of color, yet in her face line and shadow balanced between light and dark, as if between possibility—

Holgate stood still for several minutes, unable to leave.

There was a flatness to the painting—and the woman common, of perhaps forty, hair cut short, glance sidelong, look plain . . . yet Holgate saw, there and gone in her one moment no different than any other of any other woman, an entire history. Both grace, and its failing.

"Here," he spoke to himself. And thinking that if the woman were to wake into that moment it would be impossible to tell which she might find. He was unsure.

Finally, he turned and went to the gardens.

They were cool and quiet.

From them he could still see the painting.

There were trees in the garden, and bamboo, sur-rounded by small rocks and bits of whitewashed stone, and sun came from the skylight as if there were just

BIRD-SELF ACCUMULATED

that: the museum, and in it the painting and gardens and trees, and two stories above them a skylight . . . but outside and all around, no city at all.

He was the one who
clockwise from the pages of a voice or room
painted over and over again
the limit of a child's head alight in clear glass,
moving down,
yellow as rosin—

Once he'd seen a woman crawl onto the scaffolding of a billboard and fall almost dead in her sleep. The next day she was back. Another time a man got beat so bad he cried tears of blood.

Seconal drifts down the moon   faces huddled into recesses of an alley.

On the corner in front of an all night strip club, life swells exaggerated music, and a fat man with a bottle of wine dances out before some whores, telling them—do that wild thing that wild thing—shaking his two hundred and fifty pounds until he gets a smile.

Holgate walked past, looking by, paying little attention.

DON JUDSON

He went along 2nd Avenue and then cut back through the projects. They had been renamed Woodrow Wilson Estates. They were fixed up, too. A few kids rode bicycles up and down the sidewalks or played gangster in cars burnt out in front of the buildings, but mostly it was clean and quiet, and there were benches and stone chess tables and newly planted trees.

Just back of the projects was where he and Cheryl lived.

The front entranceway was locked and Holgate had left his keys on a dresser so he stepped back and counted windows and then climbed the fire escape. Theirs was the third landing up. Its screen had been left open and inside Cheryl lay in semi-darkness on the couch. Holgate walked slowly around the room touching things here and there for a minute. He couldn't help it. She'd put a cheap red and white striped plastic cover on the dining room table, and flowers in a long wine glass, and there was a calendar and many hopeful pictures of Jesus emerging from charcoal gray backgrounds to raise the dead or heal lepers while children followed behind. Holgate looked at all of this, one eye on Cheryl, fixing her there but not allowing himself to fully see, not yet, seeing instead the four or five old sketches of his she'd dug out and had framed, as if they were photographs, on tables around the room—

BIRD-SELF ACCUMULATED

thinking of her putting them out, perhaps holding herself as she sat looking. And what else? He didn't know,
not really—but allowing himself that thought for a moment, then watching the curtain rising briefly in, falling
back over the counter in the kitchen, and understanding
that this was how a thing became actual . . . because of
whatever was ordinary, because of the curtain and the
window behind it. Not felt, but drank through skin instead, half earth, half air—the ordinary taste of summer, any summer, and in *that* the rest becoming true . . .
so accepting fully then, finally, Cheryl deep blue gone
into the needle hung rather awkwardly from the crook
of her left arm.

Holgate could not be sure she was still alive.

He felt like crying, but wouldn't, instead walked
very deliberately into the kitchen and filled a towel with
ice to hold to her chest and throat.

When he was a child he'd one time come home and
found mother sat full up in a chair, bleeding from
slashes run along the inside of her forearms. She'd left
strapped to a gurney, transported through the labyrinth
corridors of Health and Rehabilitative Services, in the
end to a psychiatric unit at the city hospital. Holgate, as
a temporary state ward, was sent to a group home where
his one and only act before running away was to smash
the face of an older inmate with the first thing he could

pick up. During intake with a psychologist the doctor had wondered what sayings, such as "People who live in glass houses should never throw stones," really meant. He'd also asked Holgate to tell stories about different pictures. The pictures all looked sad to Holgate, or very tense. They'd made him think of his mother and how she'd lain, bandaged and unmoving, looking not at all like anyone's mother but instead a fat and stupid child . . . helpless really, and waiting for someone else to tell her the outcome of her situation.

"Here today, gone tomorrow," the psychologist had thrown at him.

"It's all the same," Holgate answered.

"That's it?" the psychologist had asked, and Holgate, turning then to an older inmate who'd been lounging, with a smirk on his face, by the partially opened doorway all during the interview, replied, "Fuck consequences." The older boy began laughing. Holgate went at him with a mop bucket.

After that was hiding for one month living in cars and alleys and sleeping on the tenement roof with Mr. Belenski's pigeons. "Hi, honey," his mother said when she'd finally returned, eyes blackened from God knew what.

As if he'd gone to some supermarket for a loaf of bread.

BIRD-SELF ACCUMULATED

As if her silly ass had been home forever.

Shit.

Now, with Cheryl, he did not call anyone. He held the towel to her throat. He put his shoulder under hers and half dragged her for nearly an hour from room to room, talking, prodding, begging. "Please," he asked. Please, while she dreamed a complicit life. Please, until, as she sat fully dressed in the bathtub with the shower running over her, Cheryl began to talk—she sighed and puked and then began to speak. "Goddamn" is all she'd really say. Holgate sat on the toilet hugging his knees and rocking. Cheryl smiled. She kept saying this same word over and again and shaking her head like the sound of it were truly amazing. "Goddamn," she said and Holgate couldn't tell if she were surprised or happy.

After that he considered her warily for a time, corner-eyed like an animal circling dangerous ground.

Mornings, he'd wake early and make coffee and eat sugared doughnuts over a napkin at the kitchen table, and Cheryl, sleeping late, would toss and moan in the other room. Nights, he'd begun to dream of his mother. In these dreams she was trapped beneath a frozen river. As Holgate watched, her face would balloon suddenly upward from the river bottom, blank and white, to press itself for one moment against the ice, hands pushed hopelessly before her until she was again pulled down into the current, a shadow only. He woke from these dreams drenched with sweat and frightened and would stand watching Cheryl sleep and count the thin tick of veins behind her eyelids as if their faint blue stops or starts contained the spidery web of all their lives. Holgate would touch her, everything about Cheryl painful to him, and he would lay a hand to her forehead, and walk away; and come back to touch her again . . . afraid that if she were to find him above her, frightened as she woke, he might begin to shake her, and be unable to stop.

Holgate flushed the Percodans. It was stupid, he knew, but he also took the blades from old razors and wrapped them in toilet paper and put them at the bottom of a trash can under newspaper sections and Kleenex and the cardboard backings from her makeup kits. When she went into the bathroom to run the tub three days after the overdose, finally able to walk as if it weren't necessary to test the floor before each step, or stop, leaning into walls constantly against the buzz and ringing in her ears, he told her he didn't know what had happened to them and tried to get out of going to buy more. "Use your other thing," he said.

There was a silence. He knew she was counting to ten. "Listen," she told him, "I can't use the electric razor in the tub." And the thought of that was enough to send

BIRD-SELF ACCUMULATED

him on his way to old man Yardach's where he bought a package of the plastic razors with their skinny blades built right into them. "Here," he said, throwing several through the door.

Finally, that afternoon, she'd had enough. "Go out," she told him sitting back from what seemed like their hundredth game of hi-lo-jack.

Behind her, the blinds were open and light came in and for one second she appeared not at all hollowed out by the anger that rooted and dug constantly in her mind, and Holgate wondered then what it meant to be her, how things could begin to go wrong until someone's instinct like a slow fire burned the connections of their life. "What," he asked her, confused. "What did you say?"

"Out, you know, like down the stairs and into the street. Out. Outside. The great outdoors. Gone."

He mulled this over. He said, "I don't think so."

"Bye-bye," she told him.

Holgate stared at her. She was all broken machinery—one minute fine, the next everything jumping from her face, or so fallen in she could hardly move.

"Look," she said after a pause of several beats, "okay?—I am the other adult here." Sunlight behind and spilling over, the day pinched and quiet before him.

"I am the other adult," she said, "and right now the other adult wants to sit in her house. Alone. By herself—Okay?"

She mentioned all of this like she were reciting a plan for their lives.

"I'm all right, go," she told him. "I'm great."

Holgate hesitated.

But he went outside and stood by the building's front stoop. Twice he started to climb the stairs back to the apartment, then stopped, feeling ridiculous. Fuck it, he finally decided, and walked up Telegraph Street past the strip joints and the Thai-Vietnamese restaurants. At a small market with a strobe light flashing in its window he stole a bottle of wine. The wine was cool and sweet. He wrapped it in a newspaper and held it to his thigh and crossed over to William's Point Park where Baby-Boy's uncle T.C. and a few of the other regulars were holding court. It was a beautiful day. On the road above the park's entrance cars went by, windows down, radios blasting. Holgate had the bottle of wine. What he wanted was to think about nothing at all.

"Hey," T.C. said.

Holgate sat down. "Irish Rose," he shrugged pointing to the bottle. "Vintage last fucking week." He passed it around and then T.C. brought out a bag of angel dust and right away began to explain his theory of rolling a

BIRD-SELF ACCUMULATED

perfect joint, which Holgate didn't mind as long as he demonstrated by rolling them. Besides, he was good, having been in prison hand rolling cigarettes on and off for half your life being bound to do something. And it seemed to make T.C. feel good to talk about dope. Or prison. Or anything. He considered himself, everyone knew, to be philosophical. Which was what else Holgate figured came from being locked up so long—all that time with nothing else to do but sit around and tell lies to people stupider than yourself. "Watch how I wet the end here," T.C. said, and Holgate grinned at him and the others and lay back letting them talk about whatever they wanted; and after a while it was all right, almost like he was asleep but still awake right there in the sun until the next thing he knew someone was tapping him. It was a kid. The kid was nudging Holgate with his foot and laughing, and when he saw that Holgate's eyes were open he gave a shriek and ran off.

Holgate got up.

He rinsed his mouth out with the last of the wine, breaking up a couple of hits of speed into it. Two girls were doing cartwheels nearby. They were with some people who'd set up a picnic with a cooler and sandwiches and who sat in lawn chairs watching the girls spin and spin. A breeze was coming off the lake. It was getting dark.

DON JUDSON

This is what he waited for, until his head was like rock and roll, his tongue like strips of paper.

Until girls spinning and spinning into something quite glorious.

*   *   *   *

A man from a phony adoption business comes to their apartment.

It is part of an ad run in a magazine.

Cheryl brings coffee and sits and folds her hands and smiles, nodding off, her cigarette forgotten—still trying however. Looking up when the man puts her application form on the table before him, but truly wanting only her insistent speech with the dead again.

"Melinda," she cries out, "Susan."

"Tell me," she questions, in her mind the girls stepping from a bathroom where, veined blue and dull, they had been found floating years before in a tub face down like tiny leaden dolls—"Tell me about the one thing that felt real." She has tacked blankets across the front window and laid towels, burnt yellow already at their center, over the shade of each lamp in the room. Crosses hang everywhere. Electric neon Christ above the doorway.

The man pays little attention. He is wearing a jacket

BIRD-SELF ACCUMULATED

of a material exactly cut and brushed, and when the man speaks he holds both hands at an odd angle in front of the jacket's waist as if he were fumbling to pull something from the air.

"There are," the man explains, "certain procedures."

"Payments," he says, "which must be made regardless."

Holgate watches him speak and thinks of birds pressing themselves against windows.

He can see the city, its machine of blackened buildings. And his lover. Like a memory she constructed herself into the room.

"Hopefully," the man's voice is speaking somewhere through and around her.

Although nearly ten days have passed since the robbery, Lyle still spends much of each night inside Friends Social Club watching Holgate and BabyBoy. Holgate tells everyone that Lyle is there to make sure nothing goes wrong, but even he himself does not fully believe this. He understands that something bad might happen now. It is a phrase he repeats to himself: something bad.

He says it, and the words, as if filled with unformed possibility, please him.

This is what he saw: Centeio's smile, teeth a picture

cut from magazines. *Now, and in the hour of death,* they speak, *all is calm and sane.*

He felt the night press forward.

In a living room: his mother across a broken couch. Bones sat from her skin as if she were a child sunk into itself.

Bathed in light, she could not rise.

Please, Holgate asked her.

Please.

It is almost midnight. He watches up and down the avenue for unmarked cars.

Every twenty minutes he once again ducks into an alley next to the club for more vials of crack, several of which BabyBoy immediately places inside the rolled cuff of his pant leg, the rest is pushed underneath a dumpster which sits just at the mouth of the alley.

"Got what you need," they call to people slowing, or stopping by the curb.

Holgate is aware, as if standing outside himself, of his head stitched and swollen in the glare of headlights.

At 1 A.M. he steps into Friends, and Daryl leads him to the back suite where there is an office and a floor safe and where Sydney counts money.

"Monsieur," Sydney smiles. "Monsieur Picasso?"

All business with Lyle in the club, he motions, and Holgate gives him the money and stands quietly as it is

BIRD-SELF ACCUMULATED

separated into piles and counted and banded, and then Sydney looks up, shrugging in apology to Holgate for bad manners—no tumblers of drink, no small talk—at the same time dismissing him to be led by Daryl back down through the hall and the stairs and the club itself.

Outside, Holgate smokes cigarette after cigarette.

He punches numbers into a calculator, BabyBoy working the cars—"Got what you need.

"What you need, my man," while around them the city is bled through with colors dark, then light.

Later, by three, the streets are slower, cars less frequent. Heat lightning begins to flash on and off without sound. Everything is held still as if in a photograph. Holgate and BabyBoy stand by the sidewalk in front of Friends Social Club. On the porch of a tenement next to them, an old man, awake because of the heat hallucinates a radio. He sits in a chair and rocks back and forth with a coathanger twisted around his neck. Twenty-four stations receive him up and down the coast.

Oh boys, oh girls, the old man sings softly into the coathanger's upturned end.

The summer bloodthick as if his own life.

This boy will be down.

He will be stone down.

DON JUDSON

Sydney and Daryl have put several of his drawings on a wall of their apartment. In the third floor walk-up, tight, cluttered rooms.

The fall of light, sudden across walls.

And in that can he envision once more his own witness as a boy of a fire at a horse stable—he had been with his father, it was in a state park and they'd stopped and watched—and he saw again how snow had lain across the path of the woods and laced too the air through a network of branches polished like stone. *This* the world's vast design of breath come and gone he had believed. And saw later as well, years later, long after, him going to what had become his mother's private den, and eyes closed, touching in ritual with the tip alone of a finger each cut glass figurine she had left arranged on a table, whispering in turn a name for each. . . . And thinking of both now—the day with his father, and the room and how it had been close and still—saw himself in some way suspended without connection in the two; held between one, and the other.

He wanders past rooms filled with men drinking wine from paper cups—Sydney and Daryl off to one corner. Their hushed, careful tones, the closed air.

Here is something, they would tell him.

Listen.

BIRD-SELF ACCUMULATED

During August he comes home from working the corner and drinks coffee and talks with Cheryl, and later, after he has slept, he sits alone on the front stoop. He reads almost every evening of the war going on between Centeio and the people who'd robbed him and BabyBoy.

Here is what he thinks: the city, a composition of line and angle swollen from limbs.

Bodies turn up everywhere.

One, he is pretty sure was the shotgun man himself, done in an alley next to Club Cabaret with the unmistakable Lyle signature: a single bullet wound at the back of the head, and the right hand index finger cut off neatly at its second joint. Although psychotic, Lyle is very efficient and appears capable of single-handedly carrying the day for Centeio.

And this is how he finds out about BabyBoy. Sitting on the stoop in the last sun drinking coffee sweet with sugar and thick white cream. People coming from their jobs. Later, thinking of this angers Holgate, as if their movements should have given off a clue. Gordon Davis, he reads, and ridiculously, does not immediately recognize his friend's real name. . . . Gordon Davis had been found on Atwells Avenue—a single bullet wound to the head, his right finger severed, etc. etc. Holgate puts the paper down and takes a drink of coffee. Most of the delicatessens are closing. Mom and pop corner varieties. The day remaining hot, and for some reason that is the first thing that he can think of or relate to when he realizes what has happened—Oh Christ, he says, not on a motherfucker like this. Not today.

Underneath his bed are magazines and in the magazines are pictured towns green and open, and there are ponds and paths and walks. People stand, sit, wave—all the time smiling. These are histories that can be stepped into. Holgate shows the magazines to no one. He does however show a stolen Lincoln Continental and Centeio's .45 caliber handgun to T.C.

"I don't know," T.C. says.

"Know what?"

"Shit, man."

"These people ever seen you?" Holgate begins again, listing for the third time and in precise order the reasons why it will be easy for T.C. to walk into Friends Social Club at four thirty in the morning and take from Sydney and Daryl the more than ten thousand dollars and a half pound of dope Holgate knows will be in the floor safe.

BIRD-SELF ACCUMULATED

"Put a gun in their face," he says, "can that person i.d. you?

"Is it very likely anyone unexpected will be around?"

Holgate has ten of these questions. The answer to every one is no. "Shit," T.C. says. "Oooh shit." It appears he might become ill.

When they pull up in front of Friends everything is very quiet. Holgate can hear the electric hum of the sign above the door, that and the car ticking down, but nothing else—nothing else moves. T.C. is dressed in a black warm-up suit and a foolish cowboy hat. He is holding himself very stiffly and in the silence begins breathing through his teeth and Holgate knows right then he is not going to do it.

"You know how to drive?" Holgate asks.

T.C. glares at him. "What you sayin', I'm scared? I won't go in there?"

"I'm sayin' if you know how to drive."

On the seat between them lay two empty whiskey bottles. The gun and stocking mask are in a gym bag on the floor. T.C. looks down at the bottles and then up again at Holgate. "Of course I know how to motherfucking drive."

"Good." Holgate tucks the gun into his waistband and picks up the gym bag.

Inside, everything looks different, small and out of place, like the absence of people somehow diminished the building itself. Daryl has pulled loose several of the boards from the floor in front of the bar and is standing waist deep in pipes. "What are you doing here?" he says mildly—looking up, not really surprised though, or particularly interested. He leans forward probing with a flashlight. "One of the lines got clogged," he tells Holgate who has positioned himself to stare into the mirror above the barback. Holgate raises one hand and drops it. He raises it again pointing the gun at his own reflection. "What's going on here? What the fuck are you doing?" Holgate says to himself in the mirror and then turns and shoots Daryl in the head. Sydney comes out of the office and Holgate shoots him too. Through the mouth.

T.C. and the car were gone. Holgate started toward the neighborhood, but of course he understood it to be useless, all of that was over now, so he finally turned and headed uptown. Just past dawn he took a bus, and at the first stop he got off and then caught another. After that he walked. Eventually, the sun bleached the sky of color. By then everything was without breath, and he'd already spent the better part of the afternoon

BIRD-SELF ACCUMULATED

waiting. People looked at him, a drawn young man fiercely gripping a battered grey gym bag. At four o'clock he walked into the museum with a group and then separated from them and hid himself in a bathroom. When he came out the museum was deserted. Somewhere, one of the two old men who worked as guards might be sleeping. But it didn't matter. Holgate looked at everything. In the gardens he trailed his fingers through a pool of water. A half-moon sat just above the skylight. It was as fevered as the sun had been earlier, and light from it washed the trees of bamboo or set them in shadow.

When he became tired, Holgate went to the alcove which held the painting and lay on the cool stone bench set before it.

He dreams again of someone trapped beneath ice. Only this time the face does not remain constant: it turns from that of his mother to his own. An image of himself as if encased in glass. His face blank and white. Fingers pressed beneath ice. Pressed hopelessly, reaching into the grace of one moment.